Haunted house

GREAT

STORIES

SELECTED AND
ILLUSTRATED BY
Barry Moser

Afterword by Peter Glassman

BOOKS OF WONDER • WILLIAM MORROW AND COMPANY
New York

Permission for use of the following material is gratefully acknowledged:
"Samantha and the Ghost" from Who's Afraid: And Other Strange Stories by Philippa
    Pearce. Copyright © 1981–1986 by Philippa Pearce. Reprinted by permission of
    Greenwillow Books, a division of William Morrow & Company, Inc.
"Poor Little Saturday" by Madeleine L'Engle. Copyright © 1956 by King-Size
    Publications. Reprinted by permission of Lescher & Lescher, Ltd.
"Polly Vaughn" by Barry Moser. Reprinted by permission of the author.
"The Music of Erich Zann" by H. P. Lovecraft. Reprinted by permission of Arkham House
    Publishers, Inc., and Arkham's agents, JABberwocky Literary Agency, P.O. Box 4558,
    Sunnyside, NY 11104-0558.
"Dead Aaron" by James Haskins. Reprinted by permission of the author.
"The Others" from Assignation by Joyce Carol Oates. Copyright © 1988 by The Ontario
    Review, Inc. First published by The Ecco Press in 1988. Reprinted by permission of the
    publisher.

Illustrations copyright © 1998 by Barry Moser
Afterword copyright © 1998 by Peter Glassman

Published by William Morrow and Company, Inc.
1350 Avenue of the Americas, New York, NY 10019
www.williammorrow.com
Books of Wonder
16 West Eighteenth Street, New York, NY 10011

Printed in the United States of America.

10 9 8 7 6 5 4 3 2 1

Library of Congress Cataloging-in-Publication Data
Great ghost stories / [selected by] Barry Moser.
        p. cm.—(Books of wonder)
Summary: A collection of ghost stories by such authors as H. G. Wells, Madeleine L'Engle,
        and Bram Stoker.
ISBN 0-688-14587-6
1. Ghost stories, American.   2. Ghost stories, English.   3. Children's stories, American.
4. Children's stories, English.   [1. Ghosts—Fiction.   2. Short stories.]   I. Moser, Barry.
    II. Series.   PZ5.G6974 1998   [Fic]—dc21   98-4885   CIP AC

Books of Wonder is a registered trademark of Ozma, Inc.

For my friends Ruth and Spencer Timm
with great affection
—B.M.

CONTENTS

The Monkey's Paw   9
  W. W. Jacobs

Samantha and the Ghost   26
  Philippa Pearce

The Red Room   39
  H. G. Wells

Poor Little Saturday   53
  Madeleine L'Engle

How It Happened   78
  Arthur Conan Doyle

Man-Size in Marble   84
  E. Nesbit

The Ghost   105
  Catherine Wells

Polly Vaughn   113
  Retold by Barry Moser

The Music of Erich Zann   130
    H. P. LOVECRAFT

The Judge's House   144
    BRAM STOKER

Dead Aaron   173
    RETOLD BY JAMES HASKINS

The Ghost Ship   177
    RICHARD MIDDLETON

The Others   193
    JOYCE CAROL OATES

Afterword   201

About the Authors   202

LIST OF ILLUSTRATIONS

Haunted house	*frontispiece*
The monkey's paw	*12*
A long, thin screech tore the morning quiet.	*30*
A shadow came sweeping up after me.	*44*
"I make it my profession."	*65*
We were fairly tearing down the slope.	*80*
We loved to go there, especially on bright nights.	*89*
Horrible, horrible	*111*
A pale and translucent young woman	*126*
Stark fear	*140*
A look of terrible malevolence	*158*
How that dead man could dance!	*175*
Sailing very comfortably through the windy stars	*189*
Miss Reuter	*195*

The Monkey's Paw

W. W. JACOBS

I

WITHOUT, THE NIGHT WAS COLD AND WET, but in the small parlor of Laburnum Villa the blinds were drawn and the fire burned brightly. Father and son were at chess; the former, who possessed ideas about the game involving radical changes, putting his king into such sharp and unnecessary perils that it even provoked comment from the white-haired old lady knitting placidly by the fire.

"Hark at the wind," said Mr. White, who, having seen a fatal mistake after it was too late, was amiably desirous of preventing his son from seeing it.

"I'm listening," said the latter, grimly surveying the board as he stretched out his hand. "Check."

"I should hardly think that he'd come tonight," said his father, with his hand poised over the board.

"Mate," replied the son.

"That's the worst of living so far out," bawled Mr.

White, with sudden and unlooked-for violence; "of all the beastly, slushy, out-of-the-way places to live in, this is the worst. Path's a bog, and the road's a torrent. I don't know what people are thinking about. I suppose because only two houses in the road are let, they think it doesn't matter."

"Never mind, dear," said his wife soothingly; "perhaps you'll win the next one."

Mr. White looked up sharply, just in time to intercept a knowing glance between mother and son. The words died away on his lips, and he hid a guilty grin in his thin gray beard.

"There he is," said Herbert White, as the gate banged to loudly and heavy footsteps came toward the door.

The old man rose with hospitable haste, and opening the door, was heard condoling with the new arrival. The new arrival also condoled with himself, so that Mrs. White said, "Tut, tut!" and coughed gently as her husband entered the room, followed by a tall, burly man, beady of eye and rubicund of visage.

"Sergeant Major Morris," he said, introducing him.

The sergeant major shook hands, and taking the proffered seat by the fire, watched contentedly while his host got out whisky and tumblers and stood a small copper kettle on the fire.

At the third glass his eyes got brighter, and he began to talk, the little family circle regarding with eager interest this visitor from distant parts, as he squared his broad shoulders in the chair and spoke of wild scenes and doughty deeds; of wars and plagues and strange peoples.

"Twenty-one years of it," said Mr. White, nodding at his wife and son. "When he went away he was a slip of a youth in the warehouse. Now look at him."

"He don't look to have taken much harm," said Mrs. White politely.

"I'd like to go to India myself," said the old man, "just to look round a bit, you know."

"Better where you are," said the sergeant major, shaking his head. He put down the empty glass, and sighing softly, shook it again.

"I should like to see those old temples and fakirs and jugglers," said the old man. "What was that you started telling me the other day about a monkey's paw or something, Morris?"

"Nothing," said the soldier hastily. "Leastways nothing worth hearing."

"Monkey's paw?" said Mrs. White curiously.

"Well, it's just a bit of what you might call magic, perhaps," said the sergeant major offhandedly.

His three listeners leaned forward eagerly. The visitor absentmindedly put his empty glass to his lips and then set it down again. His host filled it for him.

"To look at," said the sergeant major, fumbling in his pocket, "it's just an ordinary little paw, dried to a mummy."

He took something out of his pocket and proffered it.

Mrs. White drew back with a grimace, but her son, taking it, examined it curiously.

"And what is there special about it?" inquired Mr. White as he took it from his son, and having examined it, placed it upon the table.

"It had a spell put on it by an old fakir," said the sergeant major, "a very holy man. He wanted to show that fate ruled people's lives, and that those who interfered with it did so to their sorrow. He put a spell on it so that three separate men could each have three wishes from it."

His manner was so impressive that his hearers were conscious that their light laughter jarred somewhat.

"Well, why don't you have three, sir?" said Herbert White cleverly.

The soldier regarded him in the way that middle age is wont to regard presumptuous youth. "I have," he said quietly, and his blotchy face whitened.

"And did you really have the three wishes granted?" asked Mrs. White.

"I did," said the sergeant major, and his glass tapped against his strong teeth.

"And has anybody else wished?" persisted the old lady.

"The first man had his three wishes. Yes," was the reply; "I don't know what the first two were, but the third was for death. That's how I got the paw."

His tones were so grave that a hush fell upon the group.

"If you've had your three wishes, it's no good to you

The monkey's paw

now, then, Morris," said the old man at last. "What do you keep it for?"

The soldier shook his head. "Fancy, I suppose," he said slowly. "I did have some idea of selling it, but I don't think I will. It has caused enough mischief already. Besides, people won't buy. They think it's a fairy tale, some of them; and those who do think anything of it want to try it first and pay me afterward."

"If you could have another three wishes," said the old man, eyeing him keenly, "would you have them?"

"I don't know," said the other. "I don't know."

He took the paw, and dangling it between his forefinger and thumb, suddenly threw it upon the fire. White, with a slight cry, stooped down and snatched it off.

"Better let it burn," said the soldier solemnly.

"If you don't want it, Morris," said the other, "give it to me."

"I won't," said his friend doggedly. "I threw it on the fire. If you keep it, don't blame me for what happens. Pitch it on the fire again like a sensible man."

The other shook his head and examined his new possession closely. "How do you do it?" he inquired.

"Hold it up in your right hand and wish aloud," said the sergeant-major, "but I warn you of the consequences."

"Sounds like the *Arabian Nights*," said Mrs. White, as she rose and began to set the supper. "Don't you think you might wish for four pairs of hands for me?"

Her husband drew the talisman from his pocket, and

then all three burst into laughter as the sergeant major, with a look of alarm on his face, caught him by the arm.

"If you must wish," he said gruffly, "wish for something sensible."

Mr. White dropped it back in his pocket, and placing chairs, motioned his friend to the table. In the business of supper the talisman was partly forgotten, and afterward the three sat listening in an enthralled fashion to a second installment of the soldier's adventures in India.

"If the tale about the monkey's paw is not more truthful than those he has been telling us," said Herbert, as the door closed behind their guest, just in time to catch the last train, "we shan't make much out of it."

"Did you give him anything for it, Father?" inquired Mrs. White, regarding her husband closely.

"A trifle," said he, coloring slightly. "He didn't want it, but I made him take it. And he pressed me again to throw it away."

"Likely," said Herbert, with pretended horror. "Why, we're going to be rich, and famous, and happy. Wish to be an emperor, Father, to begin with; then you can't be hen-pecked."

He darted round the table, pursued by the maligned Mrs. White armed with an antimacassar.

Mr. White took the paw from his pocket and eyed it dubiously. "I don't know what to wish for, and that's a fact," he said slowly. "It seems to me I've got all I want."

"If you only cleared the house, you'd be quite happy,

wouldn't you!" said Herbert, with his hand on his shoulder. "Well, wish for two hundred pounds, then; that'll just do it."

His father, smiling shamefacedly at his own credulity, held up the talisman, as his son, with a solemn face, somewhat marred by a wink at his mother, sat down at the piano and struck a few impressive chords.

"I wish for two hundred pounds," said the old man distinctly.

A fine crash from the piano greeted the words, interrupted by a shuddering cry from the old man. His wife and son ran toward him.

"It moved," he cried, with a glance of disgust at the object as it lay on the floor. "As I wished, it twisted in my hand like a snake."

"Well, I don't see the money," said his son, as he picked it up and placed it on the table, "and I bet I never shall."

"It must have been your fancy, Father," said his wife, regarding him anxiously.

He shook his head. "Never mind, though; there's no harm done, but it gave me a shock all the same."

They sat down by the fire again while the two men finished their pipes. Outside, the wind was higher than ever, and the old man started nervously at the sound of a door banging upstairs. A silence unusual and depressing settled upon all three, which lasted until the old couple rose to retire for the night.

"I expect you'll find the cash tied up in a big bag in the

middle of your bed," said Herbert, as he bade them good night, "and something horrible squatting up on top of the wardrobe watching you as you pocket your ill-gotten gains."

He sat alone in the darkness, gazing at the dying fire, and seeing faces in it. The last face was so horrible and so simian that he gazed at it in amazement. It got so vivid that, with a little uneasy laugh, he felt on the table for a glass containing a little water to throw over it. His hand grasped the monkey's paw, and with a little shiver he wiped his hand on his coat and went up to bed.

II

In the brightness of the wintry sun next morning as it streamed over the breakfast table he laughed at his fears. There was an air of prosaic wholesomeness about the room which it had lacked on the previous night, and the dirty, shriveled little paw was pitched on the sideboard with a carelessness which betokened no great belief in its virtues.

"I suppose all old soldiers are the same," said Mrs. White. "The idea of our listening to such nonsense! How could wishes be granted in these days? And if they could, how could two hundred pounds hurt you, Father?"

"Might drop on his head from the sky," said the frivolous Herbert.

"Morris said the things happened so naturally," said his father, "that you might if you so wished attribute it to coincidence."

"Well, don't break into the money before I come back," said Herbert as he rose from the table. "I'm afraid it'll turn you into a mean, avaricious man, and we shall have to disown you."

His mother laughed, and following him to the door, watched him down the road; and returning to the breakfast table, was very happy at the expense of her husband's credulity. All of which did not prevent her from scurrying to the door at the postman's knock, nor prevent her from referring somewhat shortly to retired sergeant majors of bibulous habits when she found that the post brought a tailor's bill.

"Herbert will have some more of his funny remarks, I expect, when he comes home," she said, as they sat at dinner.

"I daresay," said Mr. White, pouring himself out some beer; "but for all that, the thing moved in my hand; that I'll swear to."

"You thought it did," said the old lady, soothingly.

"I say it did," replied the other. "There was no thought about it; I had just— What's the matter?"

His wife made no reply. She was watching the mysterious movements of a man outside, who, peering in an undecided fashion at the house, appeared to be trying to make up his mind to enter. In mental connection with the two hundred pounds, she noticed that the stranger was well dressed, and wore a silk hat of glossy newness. Three times he paused at the gate, and then walked on again. The fourth time he stood with his hand upon it, and then with sudden resolution flung it open and walked up the path. Mrs. White at the same moment placed her hands behind her, and hurriedly unfastening the strings of her apron, put that useful article of apparel beneath the cushion of her chair.

She brought the stranger, who seemed ill at ease, into the room. He gazed at her furtively, and listened in a pre-occupied fashion as the old lady apologized for the appearance of the room, and her husband's coat, a garment which he usually reserved for the garden. She then waited as patiently as her sex would permit for him to broach his business, but he was at first strangely silent.

"I—was asked to call," he said at last, and stooped and picked a piece of cotton from his trousers. "I come from Maw and Meggins."

The old lady started. "Is anything the matter?" she asked breathlessly. "Has anything happened to Herbert? What is it? What is it?"

Her husband interposed. "There, there, Mother," he said hastily. "Sit down, and don't jump to conclusions. You've not brought bad news, I'm sure, sir"; and he eyed the other wistfully.

"I'm sorry—" began the visitor.

"Is he hurt?" demanded the mother wildly.

The visitor bowed in assent. "Badly hurt," he said quietly, "but he is not in any pain."

"Oh, thank God!" said the old woman, clasping her hands. "Thank God for that! Thank—"

She broke off suddenly as the sinister meaning of the assurance dawned upon her and she saw the awful confirmation of her fears in the other's averted face. She caught her breath, and turning to her slower-witted husband, laid her trembling old hand upon his. There was a long silence.

"He was caught in the machinery," said the visitor at length in a low voice.

"Caught in the machinery," repeated Mr. White, in a dazed fashion, "yes."

He sat staring blankly out at the window, and taking his wife's hand between his own, pressed it as he had been wont to do in their old courting days nearly forty years before.

"He was the only one left to us," he said, turning gently to the visitor. "It is hard."

The other coughed, and rising, walked slowly to the window. "The firm wished me to convey their sincere sympathy with you in your great loss," he said, without looking round. "I beg that you will understand I am only their servant and merely obeying orders."

There was no reply; the old woman's face was white, her eyes staring, and her breath inaudible; on the husband's face was a look such as his friend the sergeant might have carried into his first action.

"I was to say that Maw and Meggins disclaim all responsibility," continued the other. "They admit no liability at all, but in consideration of your son's services, they wish to present you with a certain sum as compensation."

Mr. White dropped his wife's hand, and rising to his feet, gazed with a look of horror at his visitor. His dry lips shaped the words, "How much?"

"Two hundred pounds," was the answer.

Unconscious of his wife's shriek, the old man smiled faintly, put out his hands like a sightless man, and dropped, a senseless heap, to the floor.

III

In the huge new cemetery, some two miles distant, the old people buried their dead, and came back to the house steeped in shadow and silence. It was all over so quickly that at first they could hardly realize it, and remained in a state of expectation as though of something else to happen—something else which was to lighten this load, too heavy for old hearts to bear.

But the days passed, and expectation gave place to resignation—the hopeless resignation of the old, sometimes miscalled apathy. Sometimes they hardly exchanged a word, for now they had nothing to talk about, and their days were long to weariness.

It was about a week after that the old man, waking suddenly in the night, stretched out his hand and found himself alone. The room was in darkness, and the sound of subdued weeping came from the window. He raised himself in bed and listened.

"Come back," he said tenderly. "You will be cold."

"It is colder for my son," said the old woman, and wept afresh.

The sound of her sobs died away on his ears. The bed was warm, and his eyes heavy with sleep. He dozed fitfully, and then slept until a sudden wild cry from his wife awoke him with a start.

"The paw!" she cried wildly. "The monkey's paw!"

He started up in alarm. "Where? Where is it? What's the matter?"

She came stumbling across the room toward him. "I want it," she said quietly. "You've not destroyed it?"

"It's in the parlor, on the bracket," he replied, marveling. "Why?"

She cried and laughed together, and bending over, kissed his cheek.

"I only just thought of it," she said hysterically. "Why didn't I think of it before? Why didn't *you* think of it?"

"Think of what?" he questioned.

"The other two wishes," she replied rapidly. "We've only had one."

"Was not that enough?" he demanded fiercely.

"No," she cried triumphantly; "we'll have one more. Go down and get it quickly, and wish our boy alive again."

The man sat up in bed and flung the bedclothes from his quaking limbs. "Good God, you are mad!" he cried, aghast.

"Get it," she panted; "get it quickly, and wish— Oh, my boy, my boy!"

Her husband struck a match and lit the candle. "Get back to bed," he said unsteadily. "You don't know what you are saying."

"We had the first wish granted," said the old woman feverishly; "why not the second?"

"A coincidence," stammered the old man.

"Go and get it and wish," cried his wife, quivering with excitement.

The old man turned and regarded her, and his voice shook. "He has been dead ten days, and besides he—I would not tell you else, but—I could only recognize him by his clothing. If he was too terrible for you to see then, how now?"

"Bring him back," cried the old woman, and dragged him toward the door. "Do you think I fear the child I have nursed?"

He went down in the darkness, and felt his way to the parlor, and then to the mantelpiece. The talisman was in its place, and a horrible fear that the unspoken wish might bring his mutilated son before him ere he could escape from the room seized upon him, and he caught his breath as he found that he had lost the direction of the door. His brow cold with sweat, he felt his way round the table, and groped along the wall until he found himself in the small passage with the unwholesome thing in his hand.

Even his wife's face seemed changed as he entered the room. It was white and expectant, and to his fears seemed to have an unnatural look upon it. He was afraid of her.

"*Wish!*" she cried, in a strong voice.

"It is foolish and wicked," he faltered.

"*Wish!*" repeated his wife.

He raised his hand. "I wish my son alive again."

The talisman fell to the floor, and he regarded it fearfully. Then he sank trembling into a chair as the old woman, with burning eyes, walked to the window and raised the blind.

He sat until he was chilled with the cold, glancing occasionally at the figure of the old woman peering through the window. The candle end, which had burned below the rim of the china candlestick, was throwing pulsating shadows on the ceiling and walls, until, with a flicker larger than the rest, it expired. The old man, with an unspeakable sense of relief at the failure of the talisman, crept back to his bed, and a minute or two afterward the old woman came silently and apathetically beside him.

Neither spoke, but lay silently listening to the ticking of the clock. A stair creaked, and a squeaky mouse scurried noisily through the wall. The darkness was oppressive, and after lying for some time screwing up his courage, he took the box of matches, and striking one, went downstairs for a candle.

At the foot of the stairs the match went out, and he paused to strike another; and at the same moment a knock, so quiet and stealthy as to be scarcely audible, sounded on the front door.

The matches fell from his hand and spilled in the

passage. He stood motionless, his breath suspended until the knock was repeated. Then he turned and fled swiftly back to his room, and closed the door behind him. A third knock sounded through the house.

"What's that?" cried the old woman, starting up.

"A rat," said the old man in shaking tones—"a rat. It passed me on the stairs."

His wife sat up in bed listening. A loud knock resounded through the house.

"It's Herbert!" she screamed. "It's Herbert!"

She ran to the door, but her husband was before her, and catching her by the arm, held her tightly.

"What are you going to do?" he whispered hoarsely.

"It's my boy; it's Herbert!" she cried, struggling mechanically. "I forgot it was two miles away. What are you holding me for? Let go. I must open the door."

"For God's sake don't let it in," cried the old man, trembling.

"You're afraid of your own son," she cried, struggling. "Let me go. I'm coming, Herbert; I'm coming."

There was another knock, and another. The old woman with a sudden wrench broke free and ran from the room. Her husband followed to the landing, and called after her appealingly as she hurried downstairs. He heard the chain rattle back and the bottom bolt drawn slowly and stiffly from the socket. Then the old woman's voice, strained and panting.

"The bolt," she cried loudly. "Come down. I can't reach it."

But her husband was on his hands and knees groping wildly on the floor in search of the paw. If he could only find it before the thing outside got in. A perfect fusillade of knocks reverberated through the house, and he heard the scraping of a chair as his wife put it down in the passage against the door. He heard the creaking of the bolt as it came slowly back, and at the same moment he found the monkey's paw, and frantically breathed his third and last wish.

The knocking ceased suddenly, although the echoes of it were still in the house. He heard the chair drawn back, and the door opened. A cold wind rushed up the staircase, and a long loud wail of disappointment and misery from his wife gave him courage to run down to her side, and then to the gate beyond. The street lamp flickering opposite shone on a quiet and deserted road.

Samantha and the Ghost

PHILIPPA PEARCE

THIS WAS THE FIRST TIME that Samantha had climbed her grandparents' apple tree, and at the top she found the Ghost. After expressions of surprise on both sides, they settled sociably among the branches.

"Nice to have someone to chat to, for once," said the Ghost.

"But oughtn't you to be groaning or clanking chains?" asked Samantha.

"I'm not the groaning kind, and I haven't chains to clank," said the Ghost. "Although I do have something else, for moonlight nights."

"What?"

But the Ghost slid away from that point; he was evasive. All that Samantha could see of him in the sunlight was a wide shimmer of air over one of the outermost apple branches. If she looked directly, she could hardly be sure that he was there at all. If she focused her gaze to one side on (say) the chimney pots of her grandparents' bungalow, then—out of the corner of her eye—she could see him more clearly. Not his face, not his clothing, but an impression of a wide body and limbs. His hands seemed to be resting on his knees: was he holding something across them?

"I've never thought of an apple tree being haunted," Samantha remarked. She remembered something: "My grandfather says this tree never bears any fruit, never has any blossom even. He says it's unnatural. Well, perhaps it's because you live here."

"Possibly," said the Ghost, not interested. Samantha thought he would be interested all right if she revealed to him that her grandfather was seriously thinking of cutting down this unsatisfactory tree, to make room for raspberry canes. But she decided not to tell him that.

The Ghost said, "This tree is not my real haunt—not my original one. I was already haunting here when it was planted. You see, my bedchamber, where I first began to haunt, was here."

"Here?"

"*Here,* where the top of this apple tree now is. Our mansion was ten times the size of any of these low cottages"— he meant the bungalows, Samantha realized—"and it stood handsomely where they have now been built. My bedchamber, naturally, was on the first floor, at exactly this level: here—*here.*" The ghostly shimmer moved around in the top of the apple tree and beyond it, apparently pacing out the dimensions of a long-ago bedroom.

"And the mansion has gone—completely gone?" Samantha asked wonderingly.

"I suppose I overhaunted it," the Ghost admitted. "I made life impossible for the inhabitants."

"But, if you don't groan or clank chains or anything . . ."

"I didn't say I didn't do anything." The shimmer was seated again, and the hands moved—yes, holding something. "At first I haunted thoroughly—much more thoroughly than I have ever had the heart to do since. I haunted that house to the top of my ability. Nobody could go on living in it. Nobody. Soon the house stood empty, neglected. Woodworm abounded; dry rot set in. In the end, the thing had to be pulled down completely—razed to the ground—to make room for lesser dwellings."

"Leaving you stranded in midair," said Samantha.

"Exactly. Most awkward. There must be quite a few unfortunate spirits in my plight, up and down the country." (Samantha suddenly remembered a piercingly cold pool of air always to be passed through on a certain staircase of her school—an old ghost built into a new building, perhaps?)

The Ghost was going on: "I can tell you, I was glad when the apple tree grew up to bedchamber level. Something solid to put my feet up on at last."

"Why do you haunt a bedroom?" asked Samantha.

"I was a permanent invalid."

"I'm so sorry." Samantha had quite a tender heart. "Not bedridden, though?"

"Not entirely, but confined to the bedchamber." The Ghost sighed. "I died there."

A sad little silence, in which they heard from below the sound of the opening of the French windows of the bungalow.

Samantha's grandmother stepped into the garden. "Samantha!" She looked all round, but not upward, and Samantha made no sound. "Tea, Samantha!" She added enticingly, "And something special for tea!" She did not wait for an answer, partly because she was rather deaf, and knew it. She went back indoors, confident of Samantha's following her.

"What's special for tea?" the Ghost asked eagerly.

"I think it'll be fried sausages and bacon today." Samantha was already beginning to clamber down the tree. She paused to sniff the air. "Yes, sausages and bacon."

The Ghost was also sniffing, in a different way. He was crying, Samantha realized. Between sobs he whimpered, "Fried sausages and bacon! How I used to adore fried sausages and bacon! Bacon all curled and crisp, and sausages bursting out of their little weskits. . . ." Samantha had no idea how you comforted a ghost or lent one a handkerchief. And she hadn't a handkerchief, anyway, and she was not really sure how sympathetic she felt toward a shimmer crying its heart out over fried sausages and bacon. And her tea was waiting for her. . . .

She hardened her heart against the Ghost and jumped the last few feet to the ground. She heard, from behind her and above, the Ghost's pleading: "Come again—please, come again. . . ."

She went indoors.

After tea, Samantha spent the evening as usual with her grandparents, watching TV and playing cards. When they played, the room seemed very quiet, except for the wind moaning in the chimney and shrieking and screeching round the bungalow. "The wind's up again," said Samantha. "Like last night."

Her grandmother went on counting knitting stitches, but her grandfather began his usual complaint. He was not really a grumbler, Samantha knew, but the sound of the wind got on his nerves. He said so. "It's a ghastly sound," he said, "and it's against all reason and nature. How can the wind wail and moan and shriek *when there isn't any wind?* Time and time again, when that row starts, I've gone outside, and the air is still—still. It's unnatural."

"Unnatural . . ." Samantha repeated to herself, and remembered the barrenness of the apple tree and remembered the Ghost. . . . Suddenly it dawned on her that almost certainly she knew what object the Ghost held in his hands. She flushed with indignation.

The next morning she climbed the apple tree and tackled

A long, thin screech tore the morning quiet.

the Ghost. "You may not have chains to clank, but you have a violin and you play it at night: You play it shockingly, *horribly* badly, don't you?"

The Ghost actually seemed pleased. "So you heard my fiddling last night?"

"We couldn't help hearing you. You made my grandfather's evening a misery. Need you?"

"It's a very important part of the haunt," the Ghost said.

Before she could stop him, he had tucked the misty instrument into position under his misty chin and had drawn the bow across the strings. A long, thin screech tore the morning quiet. Down in the bungalow garden, Samantha's grandfather dropped his trowel with an exclamation of agony and clapped his hands to his ears.

"I'm sure you've no right to do that in the daytime," Samantha said sternly to the Ghost. "And why do it at all?"

"I played in life. I must do so after death."

"But why? I mean, why did you play in life? You play so abominably, you can't ever have enjoyed it."

"No," said the Ghost. "But I didn't mind it. I'm not in the least musical, you see."

"Then why—*why?*"

"I was an invalid. I needed constant attention. Constant. But after some years I found that people were losing interest in me—they were beginning to neglect to answer my bell. That's when I got myself a fiddle and began fiddling. Oh, my! They came soon enough then!" He chuckled.

"They rushed to beg me to stop. I got into the habit of fiddling instead of ringing the bell."

Samantha was looking at the Ghost with new eyes. "What was your illness?" she asked.

Again the Ghost was pleased. "Nobody knew, ever. The doctors, one and all, were baffled. Every medicine and drug and linctus and embrocation and inhalant and tablet and pill—they tried everything. In vain, in vain."

"What were the symptoms of the illness?"

"Difficult to define," said the Ghost. "Certainly lassitude."

"Lassitude?"

"Well, lethargy."

"Lethargy?"

"Don't repeat so, dear girl! Manners, manners! Yes, lassitude and lethargy: The mere notion of activity, work of any description, produced faintness, prostration, collapse. So, lassitude, lethargy—"

"Laziness," Samantha said under her breath.

"I beg your pardon?"

"Nothing. How old were you when you died?"

"A medical triumph, I suppose. I was eighty-nine. A frail eighty-nine, of course."

"How much did you weigh?"

"I really cannot see what—two hundred and thirty-eight pounds, actually."

Samantha drew a deep breath. She shouted, "You were a great, fat, lazy old pig!"

The Ghost shimmered violently with anger. "You're an ill-bred, uppish, rude little girl!"

Samantha disregarded him as though he had not spoken. "You're selfish and unkind and you've just got to stop making my grandfather's life a misery with your horrible fiddling!"

"Who says?"

"I say!"

They glared at each other.

"Get out of my tree!" said the Ghost.

"Your tree!"

"As long as my bedchamber is at the top!"

"I wouldn't stay anywhere near your silly bedroom or your stupid violin—so there!" And Samantha slid rapidly down through the branches to the ground and ran indoors. Nor did she emerge again.

That evening the screaming and shrieking round the bungalow reached an almost unbelievable pitch. Even Samantha's deaf grandmother seemed to notice it, and her grandfather grew very pale.

Samantha flung down her hand of cards and shouted: "You'll have to move house, won't you?"

"No, dear," said her grandmother.

"No," said her grandfather. "At our age, on our pensions, we can't afford to move house all over again."

"And perhaps we'll cut down the apple tree next spring," said Grandmother, "and perhaps that'll make a difference. Wind whistles through trees."

"This isn't wind," said Grandfather.

"I'm glad you'll cut the tree down, anyway," Samantha declared with savagery.

"But only if the poor thing still doesn't have any fruit blossoms next spring," said her grandmother.

They resumed their cards, playing with stony determination. Then Samantha went to bed, where she fell asleep at last to the infuriated raging of a badly played violin.

The next day was the last of Samantha's visit. Deliberately she went nowhere near the apple tree. She and her grandmother went by bus to the shops. Gently it rained.

That night they all went to bed early. There had been only a little moaning and wailing down the chimney—nothing violent. To Samantha's surprise, even this sound had died to silence. She wondered why.

Late into the night Samantha stayed awake, wondering. Almost, she was worrying. At last she got up, put on her dressing gown, tiptoed through the bungalow to the French windows, and out.

There was the apple tree, sharply defined in the moonlight, and there was the Ghost. By moonlight he and his ghostly surroundings were much more visible. He seemed to be leaning out of a window at the top of the apple tree. He was looking down at her. She was taken aback. He was, indeed, grossly fat, and very old, too, with floating white hair. But he had a babyish look that, without being exactly attractive, was at least pitiful.

"Please," he whispered down to her, "please—please come up. . . ." Samantha had, of course, been warned against strangers with strange invitations, but this one was still not very much more than a shimmer up a tree. He was no danger. She climbed up to him and they sat together, as they had done on that first—friendly—afternoon, talking. Samantha perched on a branch; the Ghost, in a long, flowered dressing gown, sat in his rocking chair by an open fire, which gave out an uncozy blaze. Round the Ghost, foggily, Samantha could see the bedchamber itself: tall windows, one of them still open; a four-poster bed; and a table whose top was crammed with medicine bottles and old-fashioned pillboxes.

"You didn't visit me today," the Ghost said reproachfully.

"I thought we'd quarreled."

"My dear girl, in life I was used to quarrels. What I never got used to—can never get used to—is being alone. Loneliness. . . ." He shed tears.

With an effort Samantha said, "I'm sorry."

"You'll visit me again tomorrow?"

"I'm afraid not. I'm going home tomorrow morning."

He burst into sobs.

Samantha could contain herself no longer. "*You* cry because you have to put up with not having a visitor, but what about my poor grandfather who has to put up with your awful, awful fiddling night after night? What about that?"

"I'd stop playing—I'd stop playing forever," wailed the Ghost, "if only I didn't have to haunt here alone, all alone. Alone for hundreds and hundreds of years. . . ."

"I'm sorry," Samantha repeated. "I go home tomorrow."

The Ghost said wistfully, "Do you think anyone else will ever climb this apple tree for a chat?"

"No."

"No?"

"Because my grandfather's going to have it chopped down next spring unless it has blossom then. And it won't do that, as long as you stay here, will it?"

"I can see what you're hinting at," said the Ghost. "You think I should leave."

Samantha said nothing.

"But how could I leave this?" He waved his arm round the misty bedroom. "I'm not fond of it, but it's all I have of home."

"Do you know," said Samantha, "you're not only a ghost, but you're haunting the mere ghost of a bedroom? That's not worthy of you."

"Isn't it?"

"No. If I were you, I'd get away. I'd go."

"But where could I go?"

"Places," Samantha said crisply.

"Have a good time, you mean? But *alone*?"

"Not alone. You said there must be lots of ghosts like yourself, stranded in midair, made more or less homeless.

Go and find them. Join up with them. Make up a party and go places."

"Really?" He was becoming excited. "Cut a dash?"

"That's it. Leave this dreary ghost of a room and all this dreary rubbish." Samantha reached forward and swept her hand dramatically over the surface of the medicine table, but her hand went through it all without effect, leaving it undisturbed.

"Allow me!" The Ghost heaved himself from his chair and waddled the few steps toward the table. He was carrying his violin in his left hand, the bow in his right. With vicious dabs of his bow, the Ghost sent bottles and boxes flying off the table in an irregular rain of medication. Samantha saw that not one of them reached the floor, because they melted into nothingness even as they fell.

The Ghost threw the bow after the bottles and boxes, and that vanished, too.

A few more waddling steps, and the Ghost was at the window. With surprising agility, he clambered up, stood on the sill—

Samantha gasped at the peril of it. But then—what peril to a ghost?

"Never again!" cried the Ghost, and flung the violin from him in a great arc. For a moment Samantha saw its shape in the moonlight; then it faded, vanished.

"And I'm off!" The Ghost flung himself forward through the window: he did not fall, he did not fly, and he certainly did not vanish. He went. He hurried through the air until he was lost to Samantha's sight. Pleasure seeking.

Samantha was left at the top of the apple tree. Round her, every trace of that ghostly bedroom had vanished with the going of the Ghost himself. She climbed down and went to bed.

The next day Samantha went home. She wrote to her grandparents to thank them for her visit, and in time she had a letter back. They reported that, oddly, the screeches and moanings round the house and down the chimney had stopped.

Samantha nodded to herself.

In the spring she visited the bungalow again. The apple tree was full of fruit blossom—a picture, as Samantha's grandmother said—and there was no question now of chopping it down.

That autumn the tree bore its first crop—a bumper one. Samantha went to help pick the apples. Her grandfather was not allowed to climb ladders, so Samantha climbed and picked. She climbed to the very top of the tree and perched there for a moment.

"What's it like up there?" called her grandfather, from below.

"Nice," said Samantha. "But a bit lonely."

The Red Room

H. G. WELLS

"I CAN ASSURE YOU," said I, "that it will take a very tangible ghost to frighten me." And I stood up before the fire with my glass in my hand.

"It is your own choosing," said the man with the withered arm, and glanced at me askance.

"Eight-and-twenty years," said I, "I have lived, and never a ghost have I seen as yet."

The old woman sat staring hard into the fire, her pale eyes wide open. "Ah," she broke in: "and eight-and-twenty years you have lived and never seen the likes of this house, I reckon. There's a many things to see, when one's still but eight-and-twenty." She swayed her head slowly from side to side. "A many things to see and sorrow for."

I half suspected the old people were trying to enhance the spiritual terrors of their house by their droning insistence. I put down my empty glass on the table and looked about the room, and caught a glimpse of myself, abbreviated and broadened to an impossible sturdiness, in the queer old mirror at the end of the room. "Well," I said, "if I see anything tonight, I shall be so much the wiser. For I come to the business with an open mind."

"It's your own choosing," said the man with the withered arm once more.

I heard the sound of a stick and a shambling step on the flags in the passage outside, and the door creaked on its hinges as a second old man entered, more bent, more wrinkled, more aged even than the first. He supported himself by a single crutch, his eyes were covered by a shade, and his lower lip, half averted, hung pale and pink from his decaying yellow teeth. He made straight for an armchair on the opposite side of the table, sat down clumsily, and began to cough. The man with the withered arm gave this newcomer a short glance of positive dislike; the old woman took no notice of his arrival, but remained with her eyes fixed steadily on the fire.

"I said—it's your own choosing," said the man with the withered arm, when the coughing had ceased for a while.

"It's my own choosing," I answered.

The man with the shade became aware of my presence for the first time, and threw his head back for a moment and sideways, to see me. I caught a momentary glimpse of his eyes, small and bright and inflamed. Then he began to cough and splutter again.

"Why don't you drink?" said the man with the withered

arm, pushing the beer towards him. The man with the shade poured out a glassful with a shaky arm that splashed half as much again on the deal table. A monstrous shadow of him crouched upon the wall and mocked his action as he poured and drank. I must confess I had scarce expected these grotesque custodians. There is to my mind something inhuman in senility, something crouching and atavistic; the human qualities seem to drop from old people insensibly day by day. The three of them made me feel uncomfortable, with their gaunt silences, their bent carriage, their evident unfriendliness to me and to one another.

"If," said I, "you will show me to this haunted room of yours, I will make myself comfortable there."

The old man with the cough jerked his head back so suddenly that it startled me, and shot another glance of his red eyes at me from under the shade; but no one answered me. I waited a minute, glancing from one to the other.

"If," I said a little louder, "if you will show me to this haunted room of yours, I will relieve you from the task of entertaining me."

"There's a candle on the slab outside the door," said the man with the withered arm, looking at my feet as he addressed me. "But if you go to the red room tonight—"

("This night of all nights!" said the old woman.)

"You go alone."

"Very well," I answered. "And which way do I go?"

"You go along the passage for a bit," said he, "until you come to a door, and through that is a spiral staircase, and halfway up that is a landing and another door covered with baize. Go through that and down the long corridor to the end, and the red room is on your left up the steps."

"Have I got that right?" I said, and repeated his directions. He corrected me in one particular.

"And are you really going?" said the man with the shade, looking at me again for the third time, with that queer, unnatural tilting of the face.

("This night of all nights!" said the old woman.)

"It is what I came for," I said, and moved towards the door. As I did so, the old man with the shade rose and staggered round the table, so as to be closer to the others and to the fire. At the door I turned and looked at them, and saw they were all close together, dark against the firelight, staring at me over their shoulders, with an intent expression on their ancient faces.

"Good night," I said, setting the door open.

"It's your own choosing," said the man with the withered arm.

I left the door wide open until the candle was well alight, and then I shut them in and walked down the chilly, echoing passage.

I must confess that the oddness of these three old pensioners in whose charge her ladyship had left the castle, and the deep-toned, old-fashioned furniture of the housekeeper's room in which they forgathered, affected me in spite of my efforts to keep myself at a matter-of-fact phase. They seemed to belong to another age, an older age, an age when things spiritual were different from this of ours, less certain; an age when omens and witches were credible, and ghosts beyond denying. Their very existence was spectral; the cut of their clothing, fashions born in dead brains. The ornaments and conveniences of the room about them were ghostly—the thoughts of vanished men, which still haunted rather than participated in the world of today. But with an effort I sent such thoughts to the right-about. The long, drafty subterranean passage was chilly and dusty, and my candle flared and made the shadows cower and quiver. The echoes rang up and down the spiral staircase, and a shadow came sweeping up after me, and one fled before me into the darkness overhead. I came to the landing and stopped there for a moment, listening to a rustling that I fancied I heard; then, satisfied of the absolute silence, I pushed open the baize-covered door and stood in the corridor.

The effect was scarcely what I expected, for the moonlight coming in by the great window on the grand staircase picked out everything in vivid black shadow or silvery illumination. Everything was in its place; the house might have been deserted on the yesterday instead of eighteen months ago. There were candles in the sockets of the sconces, and whatever dust had gathered on the carpets or upon the polished flooring was distributed so evenly as to be invisible in the moonlight. I was about to advance, and stopped abruptly. A bronze group stood upon the landing, hidden from me by the corner of the wall, but its shadow fell with marvelous distinctness upon the white paneling and gave me the impression of someone crouching to waylay me. I stood rigid for half a minute perhaps. Then, with my hand in the pocket that held my revolver, I advanced, only to discover a Ganymede and Eagle glistening in the moonlight. That incident for a time restored my nerve, and a porcelain Chinaman on a buhl table, whose head rocked silently as I passed him, scarcely startled me.

The door to the red room and the steps up to it were in a shadowy corner. I moved my candle from side to side, in order to see clearly the nature of the recess in which I stood before opening the door. Here it was, thought I, that my predecessor was found, and the memory of that story gave me a sudden twinge of apprehension. I glanced over my shoulder at the Ganymede in the moonlight, and opened the door of the red room rather hastily, with my face half-turned to the pallid silence of the landing.

I entered, closed the door behind me at once, turned the key I found in the lock within, and stood with the candle held aloft, surveying the scene of my vigil, the great red room of Lorraine Castle, in which the young duke had died. Or, rather, in which he had begun his dying, for he had opened the door and fallen headlong down the steps I

A shadow came sweeping up after me.

had just ascended. That had been the end of his vigil, of his gallant attempt to conquer the ghostly tradition of the place, and never, I thought, had apoplexy better served the ends of superstition. And there were other and older stories that clung to the room, back to the half-credible beginning of it all, the tale of a timid wife and the tragic end that came to her husband's jest of frightening her. And looking around that large somber room, with its shadowy window bays, its recesses and alcoves, one could well understand the legends that had sprouted in its black corners, its germinating darkness. My candle was a little tongue of light in its vastness, that failed to pierce the opposite end of the room, and left an ocean of mystery and suggestion beyond its island of light.

I resolved to make a systematic examination of the place at once, and dispel the fanciful suggestions of its obscurity before they obtained a hold upon me. After satisfying myself of the fastening of the door, I began to walk about the room, peering round each article of furniture, tucking up the valances of the bed, and opening its curtains wide. I pulled up the blinds and examined the fastenings of the several windows before closing the shutters, leaned forward and looked up the blackness of the wide chimney, and tapped the dark oak paneling for any secret opening. There were two big mirrors in the room, each with a pair of sconces bearing candles, and on the mantelshelf, too, were more candles in china candlesticks. All these I lit one after the other. The fire was laid—an unexpected consideration from the old housekeeper—and I lit it, to keep down any disposition to shiver, and when it was burning well, I stood round with my back to it and regarded the room again. I had pulled up a chintz-covered armchair and a table, to form a kind of barricade before me, and on this lay my revolver ready to hand. My precise examination had done me good, but I still found the remoter darkness of the place, and its perfect stillness, too stimulating for the imagination. The echoing of the stir and crackling of the fire was no sort of comfort to me. The shadow in the alcove at the end in particular had that undefinable quality of a presence, that odd suggestion of a lurking, living thing, that comes so easily in silence and solitude. At last, to reassure myself, I walked with a candle into it, and satisfied myself that there was nothing tangible there. I stood that candle upon the floor of the alcove, and left it in that position.

By this time I was in a state of considerable nervous tension, although to my reason there was no adequate cause for the condition. My mind, however, was perfectly clear. I postulated quite unreservedly that nothing supernatural could happen, and to pass the time I began to string some rhymes together, Ingoldsby fashion, of the original legend of the place. A few I spoke aloud, but the echoes were not pleasant. For the same reason I also abandoned, after a time, a conversation with myself upon the impossibility of ghosts and haunting. My mind reverted to the three old and distorted people downstairs, and I tried to keep it upon that topic. The somber reds and blacks of the room troubled me; even with seven candles the place was merely dim. The one in the alcove flared in a draft, and the fire's flickering kept the shadows and penumbra perpetually shifting and stirring. Casting about for a remedy, I recalled the candles I had seen in the passage, and, with a slight effort, walked out into the moonlight, carrying a candle and leaving the door open, and presently returned with as many as ten. These I put in various knickknacks of china with which the room was sparsely adorned, lit and placed where the shadows had lain deepest, some on the floor, some in the window recesses, until at last my seventeen candles were so arranged that not an inch of the room but had the direct light of at least one of them. It occurred to me that when the ghost came, I could warn him not to trip over them. The room was now quite brightly illuminated. There was something very cheery and reassuring in these little streaming flames, and snuffing them gave me an occupation, and afforded a helpful sense of the passage of time.

Even with that, however, the brooding expectation of the vigil weighed heavily upon me. It was after midnight that the candle in the alcove suddenly went out, and the black shadow sprang back to its place there. I did not see the candle go out; I simply turned and saw that the darkness was there, as one might start and see the unexpected presence of a stranger. "By Jove!" said I aloud. "That draft's a strong one!" And taking the matches from the table, I walked across the room in a leisurely manner to relight the corner again. My first match would not strike, and as I succeeded with the second, something seemed to blink on the wall before me. I turned my head involuntarily, and saw that the two candles on the little table by the fireplace were extinguished. I rose at once to my feet.

"Odd!" I said. "Did I do that myself in a flash of absent-mindedness?"

I walked back, relit one, and as I did so, I saw the candle in the right sconce of one of the mirrors wink and go right out, and almost immediately its companion followed it. There was no mistake about it. The flame vanished, as if the wicks had been suddenly nipped between a finger and thumb, leaving the wick neither glowing nor smoking, but black. While I stood gaping, the candle at the foot of the bed went out, and the shadows seemed to take another step towards me.

"This won't do!" said I, and first one and then another candle on the mantelshelf followed.

"What's up?" I cried, with a queer high note getting into my voice somehow. At that the candle on the wardrobe went out, and the one I had relit in the alcove followed.

"Steady on!" I said. "These candles are wanted," speaking with a half-hysterical facetiousness, and scratching away at a match the while for the mantel candlesticks. My hands trembled so much that twice I missed the rough paper of the matchbox. As the mantel emerged from darkness again, two candles in the remoter end of the window were eclipsed. But with the same match I also relit the larger mirror candles, and those on the floor near the doorway, so that for the moment I seemed to gain on the extinctions. But then in a volley there vanished four lights at once in different corners of the room, and I struck another match in quivering haste, and stood hesitating whither to take it.

As I stood undecided, an invisible hand seemed to sweep out the two candles on the table. With a cry of terror, I dashed at the alcove, then into the corner, and then into the window, relighting three, as two more vanished by the fireplace; then, perceiving a better way, I dropped the matches on the iron-bound deedbox in the corner, and caught up the bedroom candlestick. With this I avoided the delay of striking matches; but for all that the steady process of extinction went on, and the shadows I feared and fought against returned, and crept in upon me, first a step gained on this side of me and then on that. It was like a ragged storm cloud sweeping out the stars. Now and then one returned for a minute, and was lost again. I was now almost frantic with the horror of the coming darkness, and my self-possession deserted me. I leaped panting and disheveled from candle to candle in a vain struggle against that remorseless advance.

I bruised myself on the thigh against the table, I sent a chair headlong, I stumbled and fell and whisked the cloth from the table in my fall. My candle rolled away from me, and I snatched another as I rose. Abruptly this was blown out, as I swung it off the table, by the wind of my sudden movement, and immediately the two remaining candles followed. But there was light still in the room, a red light that staved off the shadows from me. The fire! Of course I could still thrust my candle between the bars and relight it!

I turned to where the flames were still dancing between the glowing coals, and splashing red reflections upon the furniture, made two steps towards the grate, and incontinently the flames dwindled and vanished, the glow vanished, the reflections rushed together and vanished, and as I thrust the candle between the bars darkness closed upon me like the shutting of an eye, wrapped about me in a stifling embrace, sealed my vision, and crushed the last vestiges of reason from my brain. The candle fell from my hand. I flung out my arms in a vain effort to thrust that ponderous blackness away from me, and, lifting up my voice, screamed with all my might—once, twice, thrice. Then I think I must have staggered to my feet. I know I thought suddenly of the moonlit corridor, and, with my head bowed and my arms over my face, made a run for the door.

But I had forgotten the exact position of the door, and struck myself heavily against the corner of the bed. I staggered back, turned, and was either struck or struck myself against some other bulky furniture. I have a vague memory of battering myself thus, to and fro in the darkness, of a cramped struggle, and of my own wild crying as I darted to and fro, of a heavy blow at last upon my forehead, a horrible sensation of falling that lasted an age, of my last frantic effort to keep my footing, and then I remember no more.

I opened my eyes in daylight. My head was roughly bandaged, and the man with the withered arm was watching my face. I looked about me, trying to remember what had happened, and for a space I could not recollect. I rolled my eyes into the corner, and saw the old woman, no longer abstracted, pouring out some drops of medicine from a little blue vial into a glass. "Where am I?" I asked. "I seem to remember you, and yet I cannot remember who you are."

They told me then, and I heard of the haunted red room as one who hears a tale. "We found you at dawn," said he, "and there was blood on your forehead and lips."

It was very slowly I recovered my memory of my experience. "You believe now," said the old man, "that the room is haunted?" He spoke no longer as one who greets an intruder, but as one who grieves for a broken friend.

"Yes," said I; "the room is haunted."

"And you have seen it. And we, who have lived here all our lives, have never set eyes upon it. Because we have never dared . . . Tell us, is it truly the old earl who—"

"No," said I; "it is not."

"I told you so," said the old lady, with the glass in her hand. "It is his poor young countess who was frightened—"

"It is not," I said. "There is neither ghost of earl nor ghost of countess in that room, there is no ghost there at all; but worse, far worse—"

"Well?" they said.

"The worst of all the things that haunt poor mortal man," said I; "and that is, in all its nakedness—*Fear!* Fear that will not have light nor sound, that will not bear with reason, that deafens and darkens and overwhelms. It followed me through the corridor, it fought against me in the room—"

I stopped abruptly. There was an interval of silence. My hand went up to my bandages.

Then the man with the shade sighed and spoke. "That is it," said he. "I knew that was it. A power of darkness. To put such a curse upon a woman! It lurks there always. You can feel it even in the daytime, even of a bright summer's day, in the hangings, in the curtains, keeping behind you however you face about. In the dusk it creeps along the corridor and follows you, so that you dare not turn. There is Fear in that room of hers—black Fear, and there will be—so long as this house of sin endures."

Poor Little Saturday
MADELEINE L'ENGLE

THE WITCH WOMAN lived in a deserted, boarded-up plantation house, and nobody knew about her but me. Nobody in the nosy little town in south Georgia where I lived when I was a boy knew that if you walked down the dusty main street to where the post office ended it, and then turned left and followed that road a piece until you got to the rusty iron gates of the drive to the plantation house, you could find goings-on would make your eyes pop out. It was just luck that I found out. Or maybe it wasn't luck at all. Maybe the witch woman wanted me to find out because of Alexandra. But now I wish I hadn't because the witch woman and Alexandra are gone forever and it's much worse than if I'd never known them.

Nobody'd lived in the plantation house since the Civil War when Colonel Londermaine was killed and Alexandra Londermaine, his beautiful young wife, hung herself on the chandelier in the ballroom. A while before I was born some northerners bought it but after a few years they stopped coming and people said it was because the house was haunted. Every few years a gang of boys or men would set out to explore the house but nobody ever found anything, and it was so well boarded up it was hard to force an entrance, so by and by the town lost interest in it. No one climbed the wall and wandered around the grounds except me.

I used to go there often during the summer because I had bad spells of malaria when sometimes I couldn't bear to lie on the iron bedstead in my room with the flies buzzing around my face, or out on the hammock on the porch with the screams and laughter of the other kids as they played torturing my ears. My aching head made it impossible for me to read, and I would drag myself down the road, scuffling my bare sunburned toes in the dust, wearing the tattered straw hat that was supposed to protect me from the heat of the sun, shivering and sweating by turns. Sometimes it would seem hours before I got to the iron gates near which the brick wall was lowest. Often I would have to lie panting on the tall prickly grass for minutes until I gathered strength to scale the wall and drop down on the other side.

But once inside the grounds it seemed cooler. One funny thing about my chills was that I didn't seem to shiver nearly as much when I could keep cool as I did at home where even the walls and the floors, if you touched them, were hot. The grounds were filled with live oaks that had grown up unchecked everywhere and afforded an almost continuous green shade. The ground was covered with ferns which were soft and cool to lie on, and when I flung myself down on my back and looked up, the roof of leaves was so thick that sometimes I couldn't see the sky at all. The sun that managed to filter through lost its bright pitiless glare and came in soft yellow shafts that didn't burn you when they touched you.

One afternoon, a scorcher early in September, which is usually our hottest month (and by then you're fagged out by the heat anyhow), I set out for the plantation. The heat lay coiled and shimmering on the road. When you looked at anything through it, it was like looking through a defective pane of glass. The dirt road was so hot that it burned even through my calloused feet and as I walked clouds of dust rose in front of me and mixed with the shimmying of the heat. I thought I'd never make the plantation. Sweat was running into my eyes but it was cold sweat, and I was shivering so that my teeth chattered as I walked. When I managed finally to fling myself down on my soft green bed of ferns inside the grounds I was seized with one of the worst chills I'd ever had in spite of the fact that my mother had given me an extra dose of quinine that morning and some 666 Malaria Medicine to boot. I shut my eyes tight and clutched the ferns with my hands and teeth to wait until the chill had passed, when I heard a soft voice call:

"Boy."

I thought at first I was delirious, because sometimes I got lightheaded when my bad attacks came on; only then I remembered that when I was delirious I didn't know it; all the strange things I saw and heard seemed perfectly natural. So when the voice said, "Boy," again, as soft and clear as the mockingbird at sunrise, I opened my eyes.

Kneeling near me on the ferns was a girl. She must have been about a year younger than I. I was almost sixteen so I guess she was fourteen or fifteen. She was dressed in a blue and white gingham dress; her face was very pale, but the kind of paleness that's supposed to be, not the sickly pale kind that was like mine showing even under the tan. Her eyes were big and very blue. Her hair was dark brown and she wore it parted in the middle in two heavy braids that were swinging in front of her shoulders as she peered into my face.

"You don't feel well, do you?" she asked. There was no trace of concern or worry in her voice. Just scientific interest.

I shook my head. "No," I whispered, almost afraid that if I talked she would vanish, because I had never seen anyone here before, and I thought that maybe I was dying because I felt so awful, and I thought maybe that gave me the power to see the ghost. But the girl in blue and white checked gingham seemed as I watched her to be good flesh and blood.

"You'd better come with me," she said. "She'll make you all right."

"Who's she?"

"Oh—just Her," she said.

My chill had begun to recede by now, so when she got up off her knees, I scrambled up, too. When she stood up her dress showed a white ruffled petticoat underneath it, and bits of green moss had left patterns on her knees and I didn't think that would happen to the knees of a ghost, so I followed her as she led the way towards the house. She did not go up the sagging, half-rotted steps which led to the veranda about whose white pillars wisteria vines climbed in wild profusion, but went around to the side of the house where there were slanting doors to a cellar. The sun and rain had long since blistered and washed off the paint, but the doors looked clean and were free of the bits of bark from the eucalyptus tree which leaned nearby and which had dropped its bits of dusty peel on either side; so I knew that these cellar stairs must frequently be used.

The girl opened the cellar doors. "You go down first," she said. I went down the cellar steps which were stone, and cool against my bare feet. As she followed me she closed the cellar doors after her and as I reached the bottom of the stairs we were in pitch darkness. I began to be very frightened until her soft voice came out of the black.

"Boy, where are you?"

"Right here."

"You'd better take my hand. You might stumble."

We reached out and found each other's hands in the darkness. Her fingers were long and cool and they closed firmly around mine. She moved with authority as though she knew her way with the familiarity born of custom.

"Poor Sat's all in the dark," she said, "but he likes it that way. He likes to sleep for weeks at a time. Sometimes he snores awfully. Sat, darling!" she called gently. A soft, bubbly, blowing sound came in answer, and she laughed happily. "Oh, Sat, you are sweet!" she said, and the bubbly sound came again. Then the girl pulled at my hand and we came out into a huge and dusty kitchen. Iron skillets, pots, and pans were still hanging on either side of the huge stove, and there was a rolling pin and a bowl of flour on the marble-topped table in the middle of the room. The girl took a lighted candle off the shelf.

"I'm going to make cookies," she said as she saw me looking at the flour and the rolling pin. She slipped her hand out of mine. "Come along." She began to walk more rapidly. We left the kitchen, crossed the hall, went through the dining room, its old mahogany table thick with dust although sheets covered the pictures on the walls. Then we went into the ballroom. The mirrors lining the walls were spotted and discolored; against one wall was a single delicate gold chair, its seat cushioned with pale rose and silver woven silk; it seemed extraordinarily well preserved. From the ceiling hung the huge chandelier from which Alexandra Londermaine had hung herself, its prisms catching and breaking up into a hundred colors the flickering of the candle and the few shafts of light that managed to slide in through the boarded-up windows. As we crossed the ballroom the girl began to dance by herself, gracefully, lightly, so that her full blue and white checked gingham skirts flew out around her. She looked at herself with pleasure in the old mirrors as she danced, the candle flaring and guttering in her right hand.

"You've stopped shaking. Now what will I tell Her?" she said as we started to climb the broad mahogany staircase. It was very dark so she took my hand again, and before we had reached the top of the stairs I obliged her by being seized by another chill. She felt my trembling fingers with satisfaction. "Oh, you've started again. That's good." She slid open one of the huge double doors at the head of the stairs.

As I looked in to what once must have been Colonel Londermaine's study I thought that surely what I saw was a scene in a dream or a vision in delirium. Seated at the huge table in the center of the room was the most extraordinary woman I had ever seen. I felt that she must be very beautiful, although she would never have fulfilled any of the standards of beauty set by our town. Even though she was seated I felt that she must be immensely tall. Piled up on the table in front of her were several huge volumes, and her finger was marking the place in the open one in front of her, but she was not reading. She was leaning back in the carved chair, her head resting against a piece of blue and gold embroidered silk that was flung across the chair back, one hand gently stroking a fawn that lay sleeping in her lap. Her eyes were closed and somehow I couldn't imagine what color they would be. It wouldn't have surprised me if they had been shining amber or the deep purple of her velvet robe. She had a great quantity of hair, the color of mahogany in firelight, which was cut quite short and seemed to be blown wildly about her head like flame. Under her closed eyes were deep shadows, and lines of pain about her mouth. Otherwise there were no marks of age on her face but I would not have been surprised to learn that she was any age in the world—a hundred, or twenty-five. Her mouth was large and mobile and she was singing something in a deep, rich voice. Two cats, one black, one white, were coiled up, each on a book, and as we opened the doors a leopard stood up quietly beside her, but did not snarl or move. It simply stood there and waited, watching us.

The girl nudged me and held her finger to her lips to warn me to be quiet, but I would not have spoken—could not, anyhow, my teeth were chattering so from my chill which I had completely forgotten, so fascinated was I by this woman sitting back with her head against the embroidered silk, soft deep sounds coming out of her throat. At last these sounds resolved themselves into words, and we listened to her as she sang. The cats slept indifferently, but the leopard listened, too:

> I sit high in my ivory tower,
>   The heavy curtains drawn.
> I've many a strange and lustrous flower,
>   A leopard and a fawn
>
> Together sleeping by my chair
>   And strange birds softly winging,
> And ever pleasant to my ear
>   Twelve maidens' voices singing.
>
> Here is my magic maps' array,
>   My mystic circle's flame.
> With symbol's art He lets me play,
>   The unknown my domain,
>
> And as I sit here in my dream
>   I see myself awake,
> Hearing a torn and bloody scream,
>   Feeling my castle shake . . .

Her song wasn't finished but she opened her eyes and looked at us. Now that his mistress knew we were here the leopard seemed ready to spring and devour me at one gulp, but she put her hand on his sapphire-studded collar to restrain him.

"Well, Alexandra," she said, "who have we here?"

The girl, who still held my hand in her long, cool fingers, answered, "It's a boy."

"So I see. Where did you find him?"

The voice sent shivers up and down my spine.

"In the fern bed. He was shaking. See? He's shaking now. Is he having a fit?" Alexandra's voice was filled with pleased interest.

"Come here, boy," the woman said.

As I didn't move, Alexandra gave me a push, and I advanced slowly. As I came near, the woman pulled one of the leopard's ears gently, saying, "Lie down, Thammuz." The beast obeyed, flinging itself at her feet. She held her hand out to me as I approached the table. If Alexandra's fingers felt firm and cool, hers had the strength of the ocean and the coolness of jade. She looked at me for a long time and I saw that her eyes were deep blue, much bluer than Alexandra's, so dark as to be almost black. When she spoke again her voice was warm and tender: "You're burning up with fever. One of the malaria bugs?" I nodded. "Well, we'll fix that for you."

When she stood and put the sleeping fawn down by the leopard, she was not as tall as I had expected her to be; nevertheless she gave an impression of great height. Several of the bookshelves in one corner were emptied of books and filled with various shaped bottles and retorts. Nearby was a large skeleton. There was an acid-stained washbasin, too; that whole section of the room looked like part of a chemist's or physicist's laboratory. She selected from among the bottles a small amber-colored one, and poured a drop of the liquid it contained into a glass of water. As the drop hit the water there was a loud hiss and clouds of dense smoke arose. When it had drifted away she handed the glass to me and said, "Drink. Drink, my boy!"

My hand was trembling so that I could scarcely hold the glass. Seeing this, she took it from me and held it to my lips.

"What is it?" I asked.

"Drink it," she said, pressing the rim of the glass against my teeth. On the first swallow I started to choke and would have pushed the stuff away, but she forced the rest of the burning liquid down my throat. My whole body felt on fire. I felt flame flickering in every vein and the room and everything in it swirled around. When I had regained my equilibrium to a certain extent I managed to gasp out again, "What is it?"

She smiled and answered:

Nine peacocks' hearts, four bats' tongues,
A pinch of moondust and a hummingbird's lungs.

Then I asked a question I would never have dared ask if

it hadn't been that I was still half drunk from the potion I had swallowed: "Are you a witch?"

She smiled again, and answered, "I make it my profession."

Since she hadn't struck me down with a flash of lightning, I went on. "Do you ride a broomstick?"

This time she laughed. "I can when I like."

"Is it—is it very hard?"

"Rather like a bucking bronco at first, but I've always been a good horsewoman, and now I can manage very nicely. I've finally progressed to sidesaddle, though I still feel safer astride. I always rode my horse astride. Still, the best witches ride sidesaddle, so . . . Now run along home. Alexandra has lessons to study and I must work. Can you hold your tongue or must I make you forget?"

"I can hold my tongue."

She looked at me and her eyes burnt into me like the potion she had given me to drink. "Yes, I think you can," she said. "Come back tomorrow if you like. Thammuz will show you out."

The leopard rose and led the way to the door. As I hesitated, unwilling to tear myself away, it came back and pulled gently but firmly on my trouser leg.

"Good-bye, boy," the witch woman said. "And you won't have any more chills and fever."

"Good-bye," I answered. I didn't say thank you. I didn't say good-bye to Alexandra. I followed the leopard out.

She let me come every day. I think she must have been

"I make it my profession."

lonely. After all I was the only thing there with a life apart from hers. And in the long run the only reason I have had a life of my own is because of her. I am as much a creation of the witch woman's as Thammuz the leopard was, or the two cats, Ashtaroth and Orus (it wasn't until many years after the last day I saw the witch woman that I learned that those were the names of the fallen angels).

She did cure my malaria, too. My parents and the towns-people thought that I had outgrown it. I grew angry when they talked about it so lightly and wanted to tell them that it was the witch woman, but I knew that if ever I breathed a word about her I would be eternally damned. Mamma thought we should write a testimonial letter to the 666 Malaria Medicine people, and maybe they'd send us a couple of dollars.

Alexandra and I became very good friends. She was a strange, aloof creature. She liked me to watch her while she danced alone in the ballroom or played on an imaginary harp—though sometimes I fancied I could hear the music. One day she took me into the drawing room and uncov-ered a portrait that was hung between two of the long boarded-up windows. Then she stepped back and held her candle high so as to throw the best light on the picture. It might have been a picture of Alexandra herself, or Alexandra as she might be in five years.

"That's my mother," she said. "Alexandra Londer-maine."

As far as I knew from the tales that went about town, Alexandra Londermaine had given birth to only one child, and that stillborn, before she had hung herself on the chandelier in the ballroom—and anyhow, any child of hers would have been Alexandra's mother or grandmother. But I didn't say anything because when Alexandra got angry she became ferocious like one of the cats, and was given to leaping on me, scratching and biting. I looked at the portrait long and silently.

"You see, she has on a ring like mine," Alexandra said, holding out her left hand, on the fourth finger of which was the most beautiful sapphire and diamond ring I had ever seen, or rather, that I could ever have imagined, for it was a ring apart from any owned by even the most wealthy of the townsfolk. Then I realized that Alexandra had brought me in here and unveiled the portrait simply that she might show me the ring to better advantage, for she had never worn a ring before.

"Where did you get it?"

"Oh, she got it for me last night."

"Alexandra," I asked suddenly, "how long have you been here?"

"Oh, a while."

"But how long?"

"Oh, I don't remember."

"But you must remember."

"I don't. I just came—like Poor Sat."

"Who's Poor Sat?" I asked, thinking for the first time of whoever it was that had made the gentle bubbly noises at Alexandra the day she found me in the fern bed.

"Why, we've never shown you Sat, have we!" she exclaimed. "I'm sure it's all right, but we'd better ask Her first."

So we went to the witch woman's room and knocked. Thammuz pulled the door open with his strong teeth and the witch woman looked up from some sort of experiment she was making with test tubes and retorts. The fawn, as usual, lay sleeping near her feet. "Well?" she said.

"Is it all right if I take him to see Poor Little Saturday?" Alexandra asked her.

"Yes, I suppose so," she answered. "But no teasing," and turned her back to us and bent again over her test tubes as Thammuz nosed us out of the room.

We went down to the cellar. Alexandra lit a lamp and took me back to the corner furthest from the doors, where there was a stall. In the stall was a two-humped camel. I couldn't help laughing as I looked at him because he grinned at Alexandra so foolishly, displaying all his huge buck teeth and blowing bubbles through them.

"She said we weren't to tease him," Alexandra said severely, rubbing her cheek against the preposterous splotchy hair that seemed to be coming out, leaving bald pink spots of skin on his long nose.

"But what—" I started.

"She rides him sometimes." Alexandra held out her hand while he nuzzled against it, scratching his rubbery lips against the diamond and sapphire of her ring. "Mostly She talks to him. She says he is very wise. He goes up to Her room sometimes and they talk and talk. I can't understand a word they say. She says it's Hindustani and Arabic. Sometimes I can remember little bits of it, like: *iderow, sorcabatcha,* and *anna bihed bech.* She says I can learn to speak with them when I finish learning French and Greek."

Poor Little Saturday was rolling his eyes in delight as Alexandra scratched behind his ears. "Why is he called Poor Little Saturday?" I asked.

Alexandra spoke with a ring of pride in her voice. "I named him. She let me."

"But why did you name him that?"

"Because he came last winter on the Saturday that was the shortest day of the year, and it rained all day so it got light later and dark earlier than it would have if it had been nice, so it really didn't have as much of itself as it should, and I felt so sorry for it I thought maybe it would feel better if we named him after it . . . She thought it was a nice name!" She turned on me suddenly.

"Oh, it is! It's a fine name!" I said quickly, smiling to myself as I realized how much greater was this compassion of Alexandra's for a day than any she might have for a human being. "How did She get him?" I asked.

"Oh, he just came."

"What do you mean?"

"She wanted him so he came. From the desert."

"He *walked*!"

"Yes. And swam part of the way. She met him at the beach and flew him here on the broomstick. You should have seen him. She was still all wet and looked so funny. She gave him hot coffee with things in it."

"What things?"

"Oh, just things."

Then the witch woman's voice came from behind us. "Well, children?"

It was the first time I had seen her out of her room. Thammuz was at her right heel, the fawn at her left. The cats, Ashtaroth and Orus, had evidently stayed upstairs. "Would you like to ride Saturday?" she asked me.

Speechless, I nodded. She put her hand against the wall and a portion of it slid down into the earth so that Poor Little Saturday was free to go out. "She's sweet, isn't she?" the witch woman asked me, looking affectionately at the strange, bumpy-kneed, splay-footed creature. "Her grandmother was very good to me in Egypt once. Besides, I love camel's milk."

"But Alexandra said she was a he!" I exclaimed.

"Alexandra's the kind of woman to whom all animals are he except cats, and all cats are she. As a matter of fact, Ashtaroth and Orus are she, but it wouldn't make any difference to Alexandra if they weren't. Go on out, Saturday. Come on!"

Saturday backed out, bumping her bulging knees and ankles against her stall, and stood under a live oak tree. "Down," the witch woman said. Saturday leered at me and didn't move. "Down, sorcabatcha!" the witch woman commanded, and Saturday obediently got down on her knees. I clambered up onto her, and before I had managed to get at all settled she rose with such a jerky motion that I knocked my chin against her front hump and nearly bit my tongue off. Round and round Saturday danced while I clung wildly to her front hump and the witch woman and Alexandra rolled on the ground with laughter. I felt as though I were on a very unseaworthy vessel on the high seas, and it wasn't long before I felt violently seasick as Saturday pranced among the live oak trees, sneezing delicately.

At last the witch woman called out, "Enough!" and Saturday stopped in her tracks, nearly throwing me, and kneeling laboriously. "It was mean to tease you," the witch woman said, pulling my nose gently. "You may come sit in my room with me for a while if you like."

There was nothing I liked better than to sit in the witch woman's room and to watch her while she studied from her books, worked out strange-looking mathematical problems, argued with the zodiac, or conducted complicated experiments with her test tubes and retorts, sometimes filling the room with sulphurous odors or flooding it with red or blue light. Only once was I afraid of her, and that was when she danced with the skeleton in the corner. She had the room flooded with a strange red glow and I almost thought I could see the flesh covering the bones of the skeleton as they danced together like lovers. I think she had forgotten that I was sitting there, half hidden in the wing chair, because when they had finished dancing and the skeleton stood in the corner again, his bones shining and polished, devoid of any living trappings, she stood with her forehead against one of the deep red velvet curtains that covered the boarded-up windows and tears streamed down her cheeks. Then she went back to her test tubes and worked feverishly. She never alluded to the incident and neither did I.

As winter drew on she let me spend more and more time in the room. Once I gathered up courage enough to ask her about herself, but I got precious little satisfaction.

"Well, then, are you maybe one of the northerners who bought the place?"

"Let's leave it at that, boy. We'll say that's who I am. Did you know that my skeleton was old Colonel Londermaine? Not so old, as a matter of fact; he was only thirty-seven when he was killed at the battle of Bunker Hill—or am I getting him confused with his great-grandfather, Rudolph Londermaine? Anyhow he was only thirty-seven, and a fine figure of a man, and Alexandra only thirty when she hung herself for love of him on the chandelier in the ball-room. Did you know that the fat man with the red mustaches has been trying to cheat your father? His cow will give sour milk for seven days. Run along now and talk to Alexandra. She's lonely."

When the winter had turned to spring and the camellias and azaleas and Cape Jessamine had given way to the more lush blooms of early May, I kissed Alexandra for the first time, very clumsily. The next evening when I managed to get away from the chores at home and hurried out to the plantation, she gave me her sapphire and diamond ring which she had swung for me on a narrow bit of turquoise satin. "It will keep us both safe," she said, "if you wear it always. And then when we're older we can get married and you can give it back to me. Only you mustn't let anyone see it, ever, ever, or She'd be very angry."

I was afraid to take the ring but when I demurred Alexandra grew furious and started kicking and biting and I had to give in.

Summer was almost over before my father discovered the ring hanging about my neck. I fought like a witch boy to keep him from pulling out the narrow ribbon and seeing the ring, and indeed the ring seemed to give me added strength and I had grown, in any case, much stronger during the winter than I had ever been in my life. But my father was still stronger than I, and he pulled it out. He looked at it in dead silence for a moment and then the storm broke. That was the famous Londermaine ring that had disappeared the night Alexandra Londermaine hung herself. That ring was worth a fortune. Where had I got it?

No one believed me when I said I had found it in the grounds near the house—I chose the grounds because I didn't want anybody to think I had been in the house or indeed that I was able to get in. I don't know why they didn't believe me; it still seems quite logical to me that I might have found it buried among the ferns.

It had been a long, dull year, and the men of the town were all bored. They took me and forced me to swallow quantities of corn liquor until I didn't know what I was saying or doing. When they had finished with me I didn't even manage to reach home before I was violently sick and then I was in my mother's arms and she was weeping over me. It was morning before I was able to slip away to the plantation house. I ran pounding up the mahogany stairs to the witch woman's room and opened the heavy sliding doors without knocking. She stood in the center of the room in her purple robe, her arms around Alexandra who was weeping bitterly. Overnight the room had completely changed. The skeleton of Colonel Londermaine was gone, and books filled the shelves in the corner of the room that had been her laboratory. Cobwebs were everywhere, and broken glass lay on the floor; dust was inches thick on her worktable. There was no sign of Thammuz, Ashtaroth, or Orus, or the fawn, but four birds were flying about her, beating their wings against her hair.

She did not look at me or in any way acknowledge my presence. Her arm about Alexandra, she led her out of the room and to the drawing room where the portrait hung. The birds followed, flying around and around them. Alexandra had stopped weeping now. Her face was very proud and pale and if she saw me miserably trailing behind them she gave no notice. When the witch woman stood in front of the portrait the sheet fell from it. She raised her arm; there was a great cloud of smoke; the smell of sulphur filled my nostrils, and when the smoke was gone, Alexandra was gone, too. Only the portrait was there, the fourth finger of the left hand now bearing no ring. The witch woman raised her hand again and the sheet lifted itself up and covered the portrait. Then she went, with the birds, slowly back to what had once been her room, and still I tailed after, frightened as I had never been before in my life, or have been since.

She stood without moving in the center of the room for a long time. At last she turned and spoke to me.

"Well, boy, where is the ring?"

"They have it."

"They made you drunk, didn't they?"

"Yes."

"I was afraid something like this would happen when I gave Alexandra the ring. But it doesn't matter . . . I'm tired . . ." She drew her hand wearily across her forehead.

"Did I—did I tell them everything?"

"You did."

"I—I didn't know."

"I know you didn't know, boy."

"Do you hate me now?"

"No, boy, I don't hate you."

"Do you have to go away?"

"Yes."

I bowed my head. "I'm so sorry. . . ."

She smiled slightly. "The sands of time . . . Cities crumble and rise and will crumble again and breath dies down and blows once more. . . ."

The birds flew madly about her head, pulling at her hair, calling into her ears. Downstairs we could hear a loud pounding, and then the crack of boards being pulled away from a window.

"Go, boy," she said to me. I stood rooted, motionless, unable to move. "GO!" she commanded, giving me a mighty push so that I stumbled out of the room. They were waiting for me by the cellar doors and caught me as I climbed out. I had to stand there and watch when they came out with her. But it wasn't the witch woman, my witch woman. It was *their* idea of a witch woman, someone thousands of years old, a disheveled old creature in rusty black, with long wisps of gray hair, a hooked nose, and four wiry black hairs springing out of the mole on her chin. Behind her flew the four birds and suddenly they went up, up, into the sky, directly in the path of the sun until they were lost in its burning glare.

Two of the men stood holding her tightly, although she wasn't struggling, but standing there, very quiet, while the others searched the house, searched it in vain. Then as a group of them went down into the cellar I remembered, and by a flicker of the old light in the witch woman's eyes I could see that she remembered, too. Poor Little Saturday had been forgotten. Out she came, prancing absurdly up the cellar steps, her rubbery lips stretched back over her gigantic teeth, her eyes bulging with terror. When she saw the witch woman, her lord and master, held captive by two dirty, insensitive men, she let out a shriek and began to kick and lunge wildly, biting, screaming with the blood-curdling, heartrending screams that only a camel can make. One of the men fell to the ground, holding a leg in which the bone had snapped from one of Saturday's kicks. The others scattered in terror, leaving the witch woman standing on the veranda supporting herself by clinging to one of the huge wisteria vines that curled around the columns. Saturday clambered up onto the veranda, and knelt while she flung herself between the two humps. Then off they ran, Saturday still screaming, her knees knocking together, the ground shaking as she pounded along. Down from the sun plummeted the four birds and flew after them.

Up and down I danced, waving my arms, shouting wildly until Saturday and the witch woman and the birds were lost in a cloud of dust, while the man with the broken leg lay moaning on the ground beside me.

How It Happened
ARTHUR CONAN DOYLE

I CAN REMEMBER some things upon that evening most distinctly, and others are like some vague, broken dreams. That is what makes it so difficult to tell a connected story. I have no idea now what it was that had taken me to London and brought me back so late. It just merges into all my other visits to London. But from the time that I got out at the little country station everything is extraordinarily clear. I can live it again—every instant of it.

I remember so well walking down the platform and looking at the illuminated clock at the end which told me that it was half-past eleven. I remember also my wondering whether I could get home before midnight. Then I remember the big motor, with its glaring headlights and litter of polished brass, waiting for me outside. It was my new thirty-horsepower Robur, which had only been delivered that day. I remember also asking Perkins, my chauffeur, how she had gone, and his saying that he thought she was excellent.

"I'll try her myself," said I, and I climbed into the driver's seat.

"The gears are not the same," said he. "Perhaps, sir, I had better drive."

"No; I should like to try her," said I.

And so we started on the five-mile drive for home.

My old car had the gears as they used always to be in notches on a bar. In this car you passed the gear lever through a gate to get on the higher ones. It was not difficult to master, and soon I thought that I understood it. It was foolish, no doubt, to begin to learn a new system in the dark, but one often does foolish things, and one has not always to pay the full price for them. I got along very well until I came to Claystall Hill. It is one of the worst hills in England, a mile and a half long and one in six in places, with three fairly sharp curves. My park gate stands at the very foot of it upon the main London road.

We were just over the brow of this hill, where the grade is steepest, when the trouble began. I had been on the top speed, and wanted to get her on the free; but she stuck between gears, and I had to get her back on the top again. By this time she was going at a great rate, so I clapped on both brakes, and one after the other they gave way. I didn't mind so much when I felt my foot brake snap, but when I put all my weight on my side brake, and the lever clanged to its full limit without a catch, it brought a cold sweat out of me. By this time we were fairly tearing down the slope. The lights were brilliant, and I brought her round the first curve all right. Then we did the second one, though it was a close shave for the ditch. There was a mile of straight then with the third curve beneath it, and after that the gate of the park. If I could shoot into that harbor all would be well, for the slope up to the house would bring her to a stand.

Perkins behaved splendidly. I should like that to be known. He was perfectly cool and alert. I had thought at the very beginning of taking the bank, and he read my intention.

"I wouldn't do it, sir," said he. "At this pace it must go over and we should have it on the top of us."

Of course he was right. He got to the electric switch and had it off, so we were in the free; but we were still running at a fearful pace. He laid his hands on the wheel.

"I'll keep her steady," said he, "if you care to jump and chance it. We can never get round that curve. Better jump, sir."

"No," said I; "I'll stick it out. You can jump if you like."

"I'll stick it with you, sir," said he.

If it had been the old car I should have jammed the gear lever into the reverse, and seen what would happen. I expect she would have stripped her gears or smashed up somehow, but it would have been a chance. As it was, I was helpless. Perkins tried to climb across, but you couldn't do it going at that pace. The wheels were whirring like a high wind and the big body creaking and groaning with the strain. But the lights were brilliant, and one could steer to

We were fairly tearing down the slope.

an inch. I remember thinking what an awful and yet majestic sight we should appear to anyone who met us. It was a narrow road, and we were just a great, roaring, golden death to anyone who came in our path.

We got round the corner with one wheel three feet high upon the bank. I thought we were surely over, but after staggering for a moment she righted and darted onwards. That was the third corner and the last one. There was only the park gate now. It was facing us, but, as luck would have it, not facing us directly. It was about twenty yards to the left up the main road into which we ran. Perhaps I could have done it, but I expect that the steering gear had been jarred when we ran on the bank. The wheel did not turn easily. We shot out of the lane. I saw the open gate on the left. I whirled round my wheel with all the strength of my wrist. Perkins and I threw our bodies across, and then the next instant, going at fifty miles an hour, my right wheel struck full on the right-hand pillar of my own gate. I heard the crash. I was conscious of flying through the air, and then—and then—!

When I became aware of my own existence once more I was among some brushwood in the shadow of the oaks upon the lodge side of the drive. A man was standing beside me. I imagined at first that it was Perkins, but when I looked again I saw that it was Stanley, a man whom I had known at college some years before, and for whom I had a really genuine affection. There was always something peculiarly sympathetic to me in Stanley's personality; and I was proud to think that I had some similar influence upon him. At the present moment I was surprised to see him, but I was like a man in a dream, giddy and shaken and quite prepared to take things as I found them without questioning them.

"What a smash!" I said. "Good Lord, what an awful smash!"

He nodded his head, and even in the gloom I could see that he was smiling the gentle, wistful smile which I connected with him.

I was quite unable to move. Indeed, I had not any desire to try to move. But my senses were exceedingly alert. I saw the wreck of the motor lit up by the moving lanterns. I saw the little group of people and heard the hushed voices. There were the lodge keeper and his wife, and one or two more. They were taking no notice of me, but were very busy round the car. Then suddenly I heard a cry of pain.

"The weight is on him. Lift it easy," cried a voice.

"It's only my leg!" said another one, which I recognized as Perkins'. "Where's master?" he cried.

"Here I am," I answered, but they did not seem to hear me. They were all bending over something which lay in front of the car.

Stanley laid his hand upon my shoulder, and his touch was inexpressibly soothing. I felt light and happy, in spite of all.

"No pain, of course?" said he.

"None," said I.

"There never is," said he.

And then suddenly a wave of amazement passed over me. Stanley! Stanley! Why, Stanley had surely died of enteric at Bloemfontein in the Boer War!

"Stanley!" I cried, and the words seemed to choke my throat. "Stanley, you are dead."

He looked at me with the same old gentle, wistful smile.

"So are you," he answered.

Man-Size in Marble

E. Nesbit

ALTHOUGH EVERY WORD OF THIS STORY is as true as despair, I do not expect people to believe it. Nowadays a "rational explanation" is required before belief is possible. Let me then, at once, offer the "rational explanation" which finds most favor among those who have heard the tale of my life's tragedy. It is held that we were "under a delusion," Laura and I, on that thirty-first of October; and that this supposition places the whole matter on a satisfactory and believable basis. The reader can judge, when he, too, has heard my story, how far this is an "explanation," and in what sense it is "rational." There were three who took part in this: Laura and I and another man. The other man still lives, and can speak to the truth of the least credible part of my story.

I never in my life knew what it was to have as much money as I required to supply the most ordinary needs—good colors, books, and cab fares—and when we were married we knew quite well that we should only be able to

live at all by "strict punctuality and attention to business."
I used to paint in those days, and Laura used to write, and
we felt sure we could keep the pot at least simmering.
Living in town was out of the question, so we went to look
for a cottage in the country, which should be at once sani-
tary and picturesque. So rarely do these two qualities meet
in one cottage that our search was for some time quite
fruitless. We tried advertisements, but most of the desirable
rural residences which we did look at proved to be lacking
in both essentials, and when a cottage chanced to have
drains it always had stucco as well and was shaped like a
tea caddy. And if we found a vine or rose-covered porch,
corruption invariably lurked within. Our minds got so
befogged by the eloquence of house agents, and the rival
disadvantages of the fever traps and outrages to beauty
which we had seen and scorned, that I very much doubt
whether either of us, on our wedding morning, knew the
difference between a house and a haystack. But when we
got away from friends and house agents, on our honeymoon, our wits grew clear again, and we knew a pretty cottage when at last we saw one. It was at Brenzett—a little
village set on a hill over against the southern marshes. We
had gone there, from the seaside village where we were
staying, to see the church, and two fields from the church
we found this cottage. It stood quite by itself, about two
miles from the village. It was a long, low building, with
rooms sticking out in unexpected places. There was a bit of
stonework—ivy-covered and moss-grown, just two old

rooms, all that was left of a big house that had once stood there—and round this stonework the house had grown up. Stripped of its roses and jasmine it would have been hideous. As it stood it was charming, and after a brief examination we took it. It was absurdly cheap. The rest of our honeymoon we spent in grubbing about in second-hand shops in the country town, picking up bits of old oak and Chippendale chairs for our furnishing. We wound up with a run up to town and a visit to Liberty's, and soon the low oak-beamed lattice-windowed rooms began to be home. There was a jolly old-fashioned garden with grass paths and no end of hollyhocks and sunflowers, and big lilies. From the window you could see the marsh pastures, and beyond them the blue, thin line of the sea. We were as happy as the summer was glorious, and settled down into work sooner than we ourselves expected. I was never tired of sketching the view and the wonderful cloud effects from the open lattice, and Laura would sit at the table and write verses about them, in which I mostly played the part of foreground.

We got a tall peasant woman to do for us. Her face and figure were good, though her cooking was of the homeliest; but she understood all about gardening, and told us all the old names of the coppices and cornfields, and the stories of the smugglers and highwaymen, and, better still, of the "things that walked," and of the "sights" which met one in lonely glens of a starlight night. She was a great comfort to us, because Laura hated housekeeping as much as I loved folklore, and we soon came to leave all the domestic business to Mrs. Dorman, and to use her legends in little magazine stories which brought in the jingling guinea.

We had three months of married happiness, and did not have a single quarrel. One October evening I had been down to smoke a pipe with the doctor—our only neighbor—a pleasant young Irishman. Laura had stayed at home to finish a comic sketch of a village episode for the *Monthly Marplot*. I left her laughing over her own jokes, and came in to find her a crumpled heap of pale muslin weeping on the window seat.

"Good heavens, my darling, what's the matter?" I cried, taking her in my arms. She leaned her little dark head against my shoulder and went on crying. I had never seen her cry before—we had always been so happy, you see—and I felt sure some frightful misfortune had happened.

"What *is* the matter? Do speak."

"It's Mrs. Dorman," she sobbed.

"What has she done?" I inquired, immensely relieved.

"She says she must go before the end of the month, and she says her niece is ill; she's gone down to see her now, but I don't believe that's the reason, because her niece is always ill. I believe someone has been setting her against us. Her manner was so queer——"

"Never mind, Pussy," I said, "whatever you do, don't cry, or I shall have to cry too, to keep you in countenance, and then you'll never respect your man again!"

She dried her eyes obediently on my handkerchief, and even smiled faintly.

"But you see," she went on, "it is really serious, because these village people are so sheepy, and if one won't do a thing you may be quite sure none of the others will. And I shall have to cook the dinners, and wash up the hateful greasy plates: and you'll have to carry cans of water about, and clean the boots and knives—and we shall never have any time for work, or earn any money, or anything. We shall have to work all day, and only be able to rest when we are waiting for the kettle to boil!"

I represented to her that even if we had to perform these duties, the day would still present some margin for other toils and recreations. But she refused to see the matter in any but the grayest light. She was very unreasonable, my Laura, but I could not have loved her any more if she had been as reasonable as Whately.

"I'll speak to Mrs. Dorman when she comes back, and see if I can't come to terms with her," I said. "Perhaps she wants a rise in her pay. It will be all right. Let's walk up to the church."

The church was a large and lonely one, and we loved to go there, especially on bright nights. The path skirted a wood, cut through it once, and ran along the crest of the hill through two meadows, and round the churchyard wall, over which the old yews loomed in black masses of shadow. This path, which was partly paved, was called "the bierbalk," for it had long been the way by which the

We loved to go there, especially on bright nights.

corpses had been carried to burial. The churchyard was richly treed, and was shadowed by great elms which stood just outside and stretched their majestic arms in benediction over the happy dead. A large, low porch let one into the building by a Norman doorway and a heavy oak door studded with iron. Inside, the arches rose into darkness, and between them the reticulated windows, which stood out white in the moonlight. In the chancel, the windows were of rich glass, which showed in faint light their noble coloring, and made the black oak of the choir pews hardly more solid than the shadows. But on each side of the altar lay a gray marble figure of a knight in full plate armor lying upon a low slab, with hands held up in everlasting prayer, and these figures, oddly enough, were always to be seen if there was any glimmer of light in the church. Their names were lost, but the peasants told of them that they had been fierce and wicked men, marauders by land and sea, who had been the scourge of their time, and had been guilty of deeds so foul that the house they had lived in—the big house, by the way, that had stood on the site of our cottage—had been stricken by lightning and the vengeance of Heaven. But for all that, the gold of their heirs had bought them a place in the church. Looking at the bad hard faces reproduced in the marble, this story was easily believed.

The church looked at its best and weirdest on that night, for the shadows of the yew trees fell through the windows upon the floor of the nave and touched the pillars with tattered shade. We sat down together without speaking, and watched the solemn beauty of the old church, with some of that awe which inspired its early builders. We walked to the chancel and looked at the sleeping warriors. Then we rested some time on the stone seat in the porch, looking out over the stretch of quiet moonlit meadows, feeling in every fiber of our beings the peace of the night and of our happy love, and came away at last with a sense that even scrubbing and black-leading were but small troubles at their worst.

Mrs. Dorman had come back from the village, and I at once invited her to a *tête-à-tête*.

"Now, Mrs. Dorman," I said, when I had got her into my painting room, "what's all this about your not staying with us?"

"I should be glad to get away, sir, before the end of the month," she answered, with her usual placid dignity.

"Have you any fault to find, Mrs. Dorman?"

"None at all, sir; you and your lady have always been most kind, I'm sure—"

"Well, what is it? Are your wages not high enough?"

"No, sir, I gets quite enough."

"Then why not stay?"

"I'd rather not"—with some hesitation—"my niece is ill."

"But your niece has been ill ever since we came."

No answer. There was a long and awkward silence. I broke it.

"Can't you stay for another month?" I asked.

"No, sir. I'm bound to go by Thursday."

And this was Monday!

"Well, I must say, I think you might have let us know before. There's no time now to get anyone else, and your mistress is not fit to do heavy housework. Can't you stay till next week?"

"I might be able to come back next week."

I was now convinced that all she wanted was a brief holiday, which we should have been willing enough to let her have, as soon as we could get a substitute.

"But why must you go this week?" I persisted. "Come, out with it."

Mrs. Dorman drew the little shawl, which she always wore, tightly across her bosom, as though she were cold. Then she said, with a sort of effort:

"They say, sir, as this was a big house in Catholic times, and there was a many deeds done here."

The nature of the "deeds" might be vaguely inferred from the inflection of Mrs. Dorman's voice—which was enough to make one's blood run cold. I was glad that Laura was not in the room. She was always nervous, as highly strung natures are, and I felt that these tales about our house, told by this old peasant woman, with her impressive manner and contagious credulity, might have made our home less dear to my wife.

"Tell me all about it, Mrs. Dorman," I said, "you needn't mind about telling me. I'm not like the young people who make fun of such things."

Which was partly true.

"Well, sir"—she sank her voice—"you may have seen in the church, beside the altar, two shapes."

"You mean the effigies of the knights in armor," I said cheerfully.

"I mean them two bodies, drawed out man-size in marble," she returned, and I had to admit that her description was a thousand times more graphic than mine, to say nothing of a certain weird force and uncanniness about the phrase "drawed out man-size in marble."

"They do say, as on All Saints' Eve them two bodies sits up on their slabs, and gets off of them, and then walks down the aisle, *in their marble*"—(another good phrase, Mrs. Dorman)—"and as the church clock strikes eleven they walks out of the church door, and over the graves, and along the bierbalk, and if it's a wet night there's the marks of their feet in the morning."

"And where do they go?" I asked, rather fascinated.

"They comes back here to their home, sir, and if anyone meets them—"

"Well, what then?" I asked.

But no—not another word could I get from her, save that her niece was ill and she must go. After what I had heard I scorned to discuss the niece, and tried to get from Mrs. Dorman more details of the legend. I could get nothing but warnings.

"Whatever you do, sir, lock the door early on All Saints' Eve, and make the cross sign over the doorstep and on the windows."

"But has anyone ever seen these things?" I persisted.

"That's not for me to say. I know what I know, sir."

"Well, who was here last year?"

"No one, sir; the lady as owned the house only stayed here in summer, and she always went to London a full month afore *the* night. And I'm sorry to inconvenience you and your lady, but my niece is ill and I must go on Thursday."

I could have shaken her for her absurd reiteration of that obvious fiction, after she had told me her real reasons.

She was determined to go, nor could our united entreaties move her in the least.

I did not tell Laura the legend of the shapes that "walked in their marble," partly because a legend concerning our house might perhaps trouble my wife, and partly, I think, from some more occult reason. This was not quite the same to me as any other story, and I did not want to talk about it till the day was over. I had very soon ceased to think of the legend, however. I was painting a portrait of Laura, against the lattice window, and I could not think of much else. I had got a splendid background of yellow and gray sunset, and was working away with enthusiasm at her face. On Thursday Mrs. Dorman went. She relented, at parting, so far as to say:

"Don't you put yourself about too much, ma'am, and if there's any little thing I can do next week, I'm sure I shan't mind."

From which I inferred that she wished to come back to

us after Halloween. Up to the last she adhered to the fiction of the niece with touching fidelity.

Thursday passed off pretty well. Laura showed marked ability in the matter of steak and potatoes, and I confess that my knives, and the plates, which I insisted upon washing, were better done than I had dared to expect.

Friday came. It is about what happened on that Friday that this is written. I wonder if I should have believed it, if anyone had told it to me. I will write the story of it as quickly and plainly as I can. Everything that happened on that day is burned into my brain. I shall not forget anything, nor leave anything out.

I got up early, I remember, and lighted the kitchen fire, and had just achieved a smoky success when my little wife came running down, as sunny and sweet as the clear October morning itself. We prepared breakfast together, and found it very good fun. The housework was soon done and when brushes and brooms and pails were quiet again, the house was still indeed. It is wonderful what a difference one makes in a house. We really missed Mrs. Dorman, quite apart from considerations concerning pots and pans. We spent the day in dusting our books and putting them straight, and dined gaily on cold steak and coffee. Laura was, if possible, brighter and gayer and sweeter than usual, and I began to think that a little domestic toil was really good for her. We had never been so merry since we were married, and the walk we had that afternoon was, I think, the happiest time of all my life. When we had watched the deep scarlet clouds slowly pale into leaden gray against a pale green sky, and saw the white mists curl up along the hedgerows in the distant marsh, we came back to the house, silently, hand in hand.

"You are sad, my darling," I said, half jestingly, as we sat down together in our little parlor. I expected a disclaimer, for my own silence had been the silence of complete happiness. To my surprise she said:

"Yes. I think I am sad, or rather I am uneasy. I don't think I'm very well. I have shivered three or four times since we came in, and it is not cold, is it?"

"No," I said, and hoped it was not a chill caught from the treacherous mists that roll up from the marshes in the dying light. No—she said, she did not think so. Then, after a silence, she spoke suddenly:

"Do you ever have presentiments of evil?"

"No," I said, smiling, "and I shouldn't believe in them if I had."

"I do," she went on. "The night my father died I knew it, though he was right away in the North of Scotland." I did not answer in words.

She sat looking at the fire for some time in silence, gently stroking my hand. At last she sprang up, came behind me, and, drawing my head back, kissed me.

"There, it's over now," she said. "What a baby I am! Come, light the candles, and we'll have some of these new Rubinstein duets."

And we spent a happy hour or two at the piano.

At about half past ten I began to long for the good-night pipe, but Laura looked so white that I felt it would be brutal of me to fill our sitting room with the fumes of strong cavendish.

"I'll take my pipe outside," I said.

"Let me come, too."

"No, sweetheart, not tonight; you're much too tired. I shan't be long. Get to bed, or I shall have an invalid to nurse tomorrow as well as the boots to clean."

I kissed her and was turning to go, when she flung her arms round my neck and held me as if she would never let me go again. I stroked her hair.

"Come, Pussy, you're overtired. The housework has been too much for you."

She loosened her clasp a little and drew a deep breath.

"No. We've been very happy today, Jack, haven't we? Don't stay out too long."

"I won't, my dearie."

I strolled out of the front door, leaving it unlatched. What a night it was! The jagged masses of heavy dark clouds were rolling at intervals from horizon to horizon, and thin white wreaths covered the stars. Through all the rush of the cloud river, the moon swam, breasting the waves and disappearing again in the darkness. When now and again her light reached the woodlands they seemed to be slowly and noiselessly waving in time to the swing of the clouds above them. There was a strange gray light over all the earth; the fields had that shadowy bloom over them which only comes from the marriage of dew and moonshine, or frost and starlight.

I walked up and down, drinking in the beauty of the quiet earth and the changing sky. The night was absolutely silent. Nothing seemed to be abroad. There was no scurrying of rabbits, or twitter of the half-asleep birds. And though the clouds went sailing across the sky, the wind that drove them never came low enough to rustle the dead leaves in the woodland paths. Across the meadows I could see the church tower standing out black and gray against the sky. I walked there thinking over our three months of happiness—and of my wife, her dear eyes, her loving ways. Oh, my little girl! My own little girl; what a vision came then of a long, glad life for you and me together!

I heard a bell-beat from the church. Eleven already! I turned to go in, but the night held me. I could not go back into our little warm rooms yet. I would go up to the church. I felt vaguely that it would be good to carry my love and thankfulness to the sanctuary whither so many loads of sorrow and gladness had been borne by the men and women of the dead years.

I looked in at the low window as I went by. Laura was half lying on her chair in front of the fire. I could not see her face, only her little head showed dark against the pale blue wall. She was quite still. Asleep, no doubt. My heart reached out to her as I went on. There must be a God, I thought, and a God Who was good. How otherwise could anything so sweet and dear as she have ever been imagined?

I walked slowly along the edge of the wood. A sound broke the stillness of the night; it was a rustling in the wood. I stopped and listened. The sound stopped too. I went on, and now distinctly heard another step than mine answer mine like an echo. It was a poacher or a wood stealer, most likely, for these were not unknown in our Arcadian neighborhood. But whoever it was, he was a fool not to step more lightly. I turned into the wood, and now the footstep seemed to come from the path I had just left. It must be an echo, I thought. The wood looked perfect in the moonlight. The large dying ferns and the brushwood showed where through thinning foliage the pale light came down. The tree trunks stood up like Gothic columns all around me. They reminded me of the church, and I turned into the bierbalk, and passed through the corpse gate between the graves to the low porch. I paused for a moment on the stone seat where Laura and I had watched the fading landscape. Then I noticed that the door of the church was open, and I blamed myself for having left it unlatched the other night. We were the only people who ever cared to come to the church except on Sundays, and I was vexed to think that through our carelessness the damp autumn airs had had a chance of getting in and injuring the old fabric. I went in. It will seem strange, perhaps, that I should have gone halfway up the aisle before I remembered—with a sudden chill, followed by as sudden a rush of self-contempt—that this was the very day and hour when, according to tradition, the "shapes drawn out man-size in marble" began to walk.

Having thus remembered the legend, and remembered it with a shiver, of which I was ashamed, I could not do otherwise than walk up toward the altar, just to look at the figures—as I said to myself; really what I wanted was to assure myself, first, that I did not believe the legend, and, secondly, that it was not true. I was rather glad that I had come. I thought now I could tell Mrs. Dorman how vain her fancies were, and how peacefully the marble figures slept on through the ghastly hour. With my hands in my pockets I passed up the aisle. In the gray dim light the eastern end of the church looked larger than usual, and the arches above the two tombs looked larger too. The moon came out and showed me the reason. I stopped short, my heart gave a leap that nearly choked me, and then sank sickeningly.

The "bodies drawn out man-size" *were gone,* and their marble slabs lay wide and bare in the vague moonlight that slanted through the east window.

Were they really gone or was I mad? Clenching my nerves, I stooped and passed my hand over the smooth slabs, and felt their flat unbroken surface. Had someone taken the things away? Was it some vile practical joke? I would make sure, anyway. In an instant I had made a torch of a newspaper, which happened to be in my pocket, and lighting it held it high above my head. Its yellow glare illu-mined the dark arches and those slabs. The figures *were* gone. And I was alone in the church; or was I alone?

And then a horror seized me, a horror indefinable and indescribable—an overwhelming certainty of supreme and accomplished calamity. I flung down the torch and tore along the aisle and out through the porch, biting my lips as I ran to keep myself from shrieking aloud. Oh, was I mad—or what was this that possessed me? I leaped the churchyard wall and took the straight cut across the fields, led by the light from our windows. Just as I got over the first stile, a dark figure seemed to spring out of the ground. Mad still with that certainty of misfortune, I made for the thing that stood in my path, shouting, "Get out of the way, can't you!"

But my push met with a more vigorous resistance than I had expected. My arms were caught just above the elbow and held as in a vice, and the raw-boned Irish doctor actually shook me.

"Would ye?" he cried, in his own unmistakable accents, "would ye, then?"

"Let me go, you fool," I gasped. "The marble figures have gone from the church; I tell you they've gone."

He broke into a ringing laugh. "I'll have to give ye a draft tomorrow, I see. Ye've bin smoking too much and lis-tening to old wives' tales."

"I tell you, I've seen the bare slabs."

"Well, come back with me. I'm going up to old

Palmer's—his daughter's ill; we'll look in at the church and let me see the bare slabs."

"You go, if you like," I said, a little less frantic for his laughter; "I'm going home to my wife."

"Rubbish, man," said he. "D'ye think I'll permit that? Are ye to go saying all yer life that ye've seen solid marble endowed with vitality, and me to go all me life saying ye were a coward? No sir—ye shan't do ut."

The night air—a human voice—and I think also the physical contact with this six feet of solid common sense, brought me back a little to my ordinary self, and the word "coward" was a mental shower bath.

"Come on, then," I said sullenly, "perhaps you're right."

He still held my arm tightly. We got over the stile and back to the church. All was still as death. The place smelt very damp and earthy. We walked up the aisle. I am not ashamed to confess that I shut my eyes: I knew the figures would not be there. I heard Kelly strike a match.

"Here they are, ye see, right enough; ye've been dreaming or drinking, asking yer pardon for the imputation."

I opened my eyes. By Kelly's expiring vesta I saw two shapes lying "in their marble" on their slabs. I drew a deep breath, and caught his hand.

"I'm awfully indebted to you," I said. "It must have been some trick of light, or I have been working rather hard, perhaps that's it. Do you know, I was quite convinced they were gone."

"I'm aware of that," he answered rather grimly. "Ye'll

have to be careful of that brain of yours, my friend, I assure ye."

He was leaning over and looking at the right-hand figure, whose stony face was the more villainous and deadly in expression.

"By Jove," he said, "something has been afoot here—this hand is broken."

And so it was. I was certain that it had been perfect the last time Laura and I had been there.

"Perhaps someone has *tried* to remove them," said the young doctor.

"That won't account for my impression," I objected.

"Too much painting and tobacco will account for that, well enough."

"Come along," I said, "or my wife will be getting anxious. You'll come in and have a drop of whiskey and drink confusion to ghosts and better sense to me."

"I ought to go up to Palmer's, but it's so late now I'd best leave it till the morning," he replied. "I was kept late at the Union, and I've had to see a lot of people since. All right, I'll come back with ye."

I think he fancied I needed him more than did Palmer's girl, so, discussing how such an illusion could have been possible, and deducing from this experience large generalities concerning ghostly apparitions, we walked up to our cottage. We saw, as we walked up the garden path, that bright light streamed out of the front door, and presently saw that the parlor door was open too. Had she gone out?

"Come in," I said, and Dr. Kelly followed me into the parlor. It was all ablaze with candles, not only the wax ones, but at least a dozen guttering, glaring tallow dips, stuck in vases and ornaments in unlikely places. Light, I knew, was Laura's remedy for nervousness. Poor child! Why had I left her? Brute that I was.

We glanced round the room, and at first we did not see her. The window was open, and the draft set all the candles flaring one way. Her chair was empty and her handkerchief and book lay on the floor. I turned to the window. There, in the recess of the window, I saw her. Oh, my child, my love, had she gone to that window to watch for me? And what had come into the room behind her? To what had she turned with that look of frantic fear and horror? Oh, my little one, had she thought that it was I whose step she heard, and turned to meet—what?

She had fallen back across a table in the window, and her body lay half on it and half on the window seat, and her head hung down over the table, the brown hair loosened and fallen to the carpet. Her lips were drawn back, and her eyes wide, wide open. They saw nothing now. What had they seen last?

The doctor moved towards her, but I pushed him aside and sprang to her, caught her in my arms and cried:

"It's all right, Laura! I've got you safe, wifie."

She fell into my arms in a heap. I clasped her and kissed

her, and called her by all her pet names, but I think I knew all the time that she was dead. Her hands were tightly clenched. In one of them she held something fast. When I was quite sure that she was dead, and that nothing mattered at all anymore, I let him open her hand to see what she held.

It was a gray marble finger.

The Ghost

CATHERINE WELLS

SHE WAS A GIRL OF FOURTEEN, and she sat propped up with pillows in an old four-poster bed, coughing a little with the feverish cold that kept her there. She was tired of reading by lamplight, and she lay and listened to the few sounds that she could hear, and looked into the fire. From downstairs, down the wide, rather dark, oak-paneled corridor hung with brown ocher pictures of tremendous naval engagements exploding fierily in their centers, down the broad stone stairs that ended in a heavy, creaking, nail-studded door, there blew in to her remoteness sometimes a gust of dance music. Cousins and cousins and cousins were down there, and Uncle Timothy, as host, leading the fun. Several of them had danced into her room during the day, and said that her illness was a "perfect shame," told her that the skating in the park was "too heavenly," and danced out again. Uncle Timothy had been as kind as kind could be. But—downstairs all the full cup of happiness the lonely child had looked forward to so eagerly for a month was running away like liquid gold.

She watched the flames of the big wood fire in the open grate flicker and fall. She had sometimes to clench her hands to prevent herself from crying. She had discovered— so early was she beginning to collect her little stock of feminine lore—that if you swallowed hard and rapidly as the tears gathered, that you could prevent your eyes brimming over. She wished someone would come. There was a bell within her reach, but she could think of no plausible excuse for ringing it. She wished there was more light in the room. The big fire lit it up cheerfully when the logs flared high; but when they only glowed, the dark shadows crept down from the ceiling and gathered in the corners against the paneling. She turned from the scrutiny of the room to the bright circle of light under the lamp on the table beside her, and the companionable suggestiveness of the currant jelly and spoon, grapes and lemonade and little pile of books and kindly fuss that shone warmly and comfortingly there. Perhaps it would not be long before Mrs. Bunting, her uncle's housekeeper, would come in again and sit down and talk to her.

Mrs. Bunting, very probably, was more occupied than usual that evening. There were several extra guests; another house party had motored over for the evening, and they had brought with them a romantic figure, a celebrity, no less a personage than the actor Percival East. The girl had indeed broken down from her fortitude that afternoon when Uncle Timothy had told her of this visitor. Uncle Timothy was surprised; it was only another schoolgirl who would have understood fully what it meant to be denied by a mere cold the chance of meeting face to face that chivalrous hero of drama; another girl who had glowed at his daring, wept at his noble renunciations, been made happy, albeit enviously and vicariously, by his final embrace with the lady of his love.

"There, there, dear child," Uncle Timothy had said, patting her shoulder and greatly distressed. "Never mind, never mind. If you can't get up I'll bring him in to see you here. I promise I will. . . . But the *pull* these chaps have over you little women," he went on, half to himself. . . .

The paneling creaked. Of course, it always did in these old houses. She was of that order of apprehensive, slightly nervous people who do not believe in ghosts, but all the same hope devoutly they may never see one. Surely it was a long time since anyone had visited her; it would be hours, she supposed, before the girl who had the room next her own, into which a communicating door comfortingly led, came up to bed. If she rang it took a minute or two before anyone reached her from the remote servants' quarters. There ought soon, she thought, to be a housemaid about the corridor outside, tidying up the bedrooms, putting coal on the fires, and making suchlike companionable noises. That would be pleasant. How bored one got in bed anyhow, and how dreadful it was, how unbearably dreadful it was that she should be stuck in bed now, missing everything, missing every bit of the glorious glowing time that was slipping away down there. At that she had to begin swallowing her tears again.

With a sudden burst of sound, a storm of clapping and laughter, the heavy door at the foot of the big stairs swung open and closed. Footsteps came upstairs, and she heard men's voices approaching. Uncle Timothy. He knocked at the door ajar. "Come in," she cried gladly. With him was a quiet-faced grayish-haired man of middle age. Then uncle had sent for the doctor after all!

"Here is another of your young worshipers, Mr. East," said Uncle Timothy.

Mr. East! She realized in a flash that she had expected him in purple brocade, powdered hair, and ruffles of fine lace. Her uncle smiled at her disconcerted face.

"She doesn't seem to recognize you, Mr. East," said Uncle Timothy.

"Of course I do," she declared bravely, and sat up, flushed with excitement and her feverishness, bright-eyed and with ruffled hair. Indeed she began to see the stage hero she remembered and the kindly-faced man before her flow together like a composite portrait. There was the little nod of the head, there was the chin, yes! and the eyes, now she came to look at them. "Why were they all clapping you?" she asked.

"Because I had just promised to frighten them out of their wits," replied Mr. East.

"Oh, how?"

"Mr. East," said Uncle Timothy, "is going to dress up as our long-lost ghost, and give us a really shuddering time of it downstairs."

"*Are* you?" cried the girl with all the fierce desire that only a girl can utter in her voice. "Oh, why am I ill like this, Uncle Timothy? I'm not ill really. Can't you see I'm better? I've been in bed all day. I'm perfectly well. Can't I come down, Uncle *dear*—can't I?"

In her excitement she was half out of bed. "There, there, child," soothed Uncle Timothy, hastily smoothing the bed-clothes and trying to tuck her in.

"But *can't* I?"

"Of course, if you want to be thoroughly frightened, frightened out of your wits, mind you," began Percival East.

"I do, I *do*," she cried, bouncing up and down in her bed.

"I'll come and show myself when I'm dressed up, before I go down."

"Oh please, please," she cried back radiantly. A private performance all to herself! "Will you be perfectly *awful*?" she laughed exultantly.

"As ever I can," smiled Mr. East, and turned to follow Uncle Timothy out of the room. "You know," he said, holding the door and looking back at her with mock seriousness, "I shall look rather horrid, I expect. Are you sure you won't mind?"

"*Mind*—when it's you?" laughed the girl.

He went out of the room, shutting the door.

"Rum-ti-tum, ti-tum, ti-ty," she hummed gaily, and wriggled down into her bedclothes again, straightened the sheet over her chest, and prepared to wait.

She lay quietly for some time, with a smile on her face, thinking of Percival East and fitting his grave, kindly face back into its various dramatic settings. She was quite satisfied with him. She began to go over in her mind in detail the last play in which she had seen him act. How splendid he had looked when he fought the duel! She couldn't imagine him gruesome, she thought. What would he do with himself?

Whatever he did, she wasn't going to be frightened. He shouldn't be able to boast he had frightened *her.* Uncle Timothy would be there too, she supposed. Would he?

Footsteps went past her door outside, along the corridor, and died away. The big door at the end of the stairs opened and clanged shut.

Uncle Timothy had gone down.

She waited on.

A log, burnt through the middle to a ruddy thread, fell suddenly in two tumbling pieces on the hearth. She started at the sound. How quiet everything was. How much longer would he be, she wondered. The fire wanted making up, the pieces of wood collecting together. Should she ring? But he might come in just when the servant was mending the fire, and that would spoil his entry. The fire could wait. . . .

Horrible, horrible

The room was very still, and, with the fallen fire, darker. She heard no more any sound at all from downstairs. That was because her door was shut. All day it had been open, but now the last slender link that held her to downstairs was broken.

The lamp flame gave a sudden fitful leap. Why? Was it going out? Was it—? No.

She hoped he wouldn't jump out at her, but of course he wouldn't. Anyhow, whatever he did she wouldn't be frightened—really frightened. Forewarned is forearmed.

Was that a sound? She started up, her eyes on the door. Nothing.

But surely, the door had minutely moved, it did not sit back quite so close into its frame! Perhaps it— She was sure it had moved. Yes, it had moved—opened an inch, and slowly, as she watched, she saw a thread of light grow between the edge of the door and its frame, grow almost imperceptibly wider, and stop.

He could never come through that. It must have yawned open of its own accord. Her heart began to beat rather quickly. She could see only the upper part of the door; the foot of her bed hid the lower third. . . .

Her attention tightened. Suddenly, as suddenly as a pistol shot, she saw that there was a little figure like a dwarf near the wall, between the door and the fireplace. It was a little cloaked figure, no higher than the table. How *did* he do it? It was moving slowly, very slowly, towards the fire, as if it was quite unconscious of her; it was wrapped about in a cloak that trailed, with a slouched hat on its head bent down to its shoulders. She gripped the clothes with her hands, it was so queer, so unexpected; she gave a little gasping laugh to break the tension of the silence—to show she appreciated him.

The dwarf stopped dead at the sound, and turned its face round to her.

Oh! But she was frightened! It was a dead white face, a long pointed face hunched between its shoulders; there was no color in the eyes that stared at her! How did he do it, how *did* he do it? It was too good. She laughed again nervously, and with a clutch of terror that she could not control she saw the creature move out of the shadow and come towards her. She braced herself with all her might; she mustn't be frightened by a bit of acting—he was coming nearer, it was horrible, horrible—right up to her bed. . . .

She flung her head beneath her bedclothes. Whether she screamed or not she never knew. . . .

Someone was rapping at her door, speaking cheerily. She took her head out of the clothes with a revulsion of shame at her fright. The horrible little creature was gone! Mr. East was speaking at her door. What was it he was saying? *What?*

"I'm ready now," he said. *"Shall I come in, and begin?"*

Polly Vaughn

A Traditional British Ballad
RETOLD BY BARRY MOSER

POLLY AND JIMMY WERE SWEETHEARTS. Had been since they were kids in "kinleygarten." All the boys liked Polly. The girls did, too. But of all her friends Polly liked Jimmy Randall best. And he liked her best. She called him "Jimmer" and he called her "Pol." They were sweethearts up to the tenth grade, when Jimmy quit school to go to work in the coal mines. They were sweethearts after that, too, and were to be married on Polly's twentieth birthday, which was two weeks away.

Polly and her mother were making dresses and were busy sewing and trying them on. Polly looked pretty in her white dress, even though there was nothing special about her looks except a quick, warm smile and her long, fawn-colored hair. It was her kind nature and generous spirit that everybody loved so much. "She's such a *sweet* chile," was what everybody said about her. She was as kind and sweet to strangers and animals as she was to her own family. She loved animals of all kinds. She brought home sick and hurt animals so often that her mother would say, "I declare, that chile loves animals more than she does folks."

Polly and her family lived halfway up Cold Iron Mountain in a cabin that had been in her family for four generations. Polly's daddy, Merle Vaughn, worked in the Stone Creek Mines just like his daddy and granddaddy had. He stayed inside most all the time—inside the mines, inside the house, and inside himself. Polly's momma, Bessie Joyce, was a stout woman, and real talkative. She and Polly talked all the time—about what book Polly was reading and about the wedding and about the cabin Polly and Jimmy were planning to build. Every year Bessie Joyce put in a truck garden that was as pretty as a picture. She looked after the cows and pigs, too, and raised all the children—Polly and her two brothers and three sisters: Lottie and Anna Belle, Truman and John Delmar, and the baby, Florinda.

Jimmy was a sweet kid, too, and most everybody liked him. He had always been shy and, like Polly, nothing special to look at. He had a shock of red hair and a mess of freckles all over his nose. As a boy he liked to play softball and he liked to shoot marbles. He played ball with the boys, but he shot marbles with Polly. He'd just smile and go on about his business when the boys kidded him for playing with Polly. But she could shoot Rolley Hole better than any of them—and besides that, she had her own bag of flint marbles.

Even when they weren't in school, Polly and Jimmy spent a lot of time together—swinging in the swing on Polly's front porch, shooting Rolley Hole, or playing Old Maid. Most of all, though, they walked in the woods together. Polly wasn't afraid of snakes or lizards or tadpoles or anything. She'd go places he wouldn't go, she saw things that he didn't see, and she knew things he didn't know—the names of plants and animals and birds and insects. She even knew which mushrooms and roots you could eat. Jimmy's folks didn't eat things like that—they ate pork and venison, corn and collard greens, and potatoes and johnnycake.

Jimmy's folks kept pretty much to themselves. When the Randalls moved to Cold Iron Mountain, back in 1907, Merle Vaughn claimed that the Randalls had gone and built their cabin on Vaughn land. There was a big dispute, and Merle nailed a sign up in the woods warning "all Randalls and all other liars" not to set foot on his land, else he'd shoot them. Merle Vaughn had held a grudge against the Randalls ever since.

Jewett Randall worked in the Stone Creek Mines, too, though nowhere near Merle Vaughn. The only friends Jewett Randall had were his family. He was an irascible man, Jewett—always a bad mood, always a mean tongue, and always quick to fight. Some said that they believed old Jewett kind of liked the dispute over the land. Said it "give him something to be mad about" all the time. Then again, Jewett didn't like people any better than they liked him. About the only things he did like were his family and hunting, and, my, how that man loved hunting—rabbits, wild turkeys, black bears, partridges, pigeons—it didn't matter to Jewett Randall what he hunted or where he hunted it. Deer hunting, though, was special in the Randall family. Like in most of the families on Cold Iron Mountain, it was a way of life. It was what they talked about sitting on the porch. It was what they talked about sitting at the dinner table. It was what they talked about sitting around the fire.

Jimmy was ten when he killed his first deer, a doe. It was early spring, out of season. Jimmy didn't even want to go that morning. He was going over to play with Polly, but his daddy and his brother, Lester, teased him about playing with girls, so Jimmy went along. There were patches of snow still hiding behind rocks and beneath trees, and when the doe sprang over the fence, Jimmy saw her white tail flash in the morning sunlight. He pointed his gun and shot—not thinking, really, just hoping to please his daddy and impress his big brother. It wasn't a clean shot. She fell into the fence and tangled her hind leg in the barbed wire. Jimmy had to shoot her again, up close, to put her out of her misery. Jimmy hated that. His daddy told him it was all right, "'cause it had to be done," and anyway, he said, "a doe tastes jest as good as a buck does. It's jest too bad ya shot when ya did, son, 'cause yer brother Lester here had a big eight-point buck in his sights jest as ya fired, and he done got away clean. Boy! Them antlers shore would've looked mighty han'some over the mantelpiece." Jewett and Lester hung the doe by her hocks on a meat pole and tried to get Jimmy to gut her, but Jimmy wouldn't do it. So his daddy did it for him. And when he did, the doe's entrails spilled out warm and steaming on the cold ground. Jewett cupped his hand in some of her blood and smeared it on Jimmy's face. That's what men do to celebrate a boy's first kill. To Jewett and Lester, Jimmy was a man. But Jimmy didn't feel any different—all he felt was a little sick to his stomach. Jimmy never cared for hunting after that.

Merle Vaughn said he wasn't going to go to the wedding, but Polly and her mama weren't concerned—they figured he'd change his mind. They were happy and excited as they put the final touches of lace on Polly's dress. That afternoon, when they finished, Polly went out for a walk in the woods. She pulled on a pair of old coveralls—right over her favorite blouse, a white cotton one with a lace collar. Polly loved lace. She had taught herself to make "poor man's lace" years ago when she had chicken pox and had to stay home from school for two weeks. She had tatted a good deal of it for her wedding dress. When she left the house she put on a buckskin jacket that Jimmy's mother,

Eulalia, had made for her from the hide of a deer that Jimmy's brother had killed. Polly didn't like it that the Randalls hunted deer; she was glad that her daddy and brothers and Jimmy didn't like hunting. Jimmy had told Polly that all he liked about hunting was getting out in the woods with his family and friends. He told her that sometimes he'd shoot wide, missing his target on purpose, and that sometimes he'd shoot at nothing at all just to scare things away—except, of course, when the family needed something to eat. Nonetheless, Polly was glad she had the jacket on because it was warm and it protected her lace from prickers and thorns.

Jimmy was in the woods, too, that November afternoon. He was taking a shortcut over to the Vaughn place to meet Polly and go to Sunday evening prayer meeting with her. He had gone only a few feet from the cabin when his mama hollered at him: "Take yer gun with ya, Jimmy—jest in case ya see som'thin', honey—God knows we shore could use some fresh meat." So Jimmy went back to the cabin and fetched his gun.

He was nearing the old Wilhoit Bridge when he heard something rustling in the bushes on the other side of the creek.

Polly was gathering gentian when she heard footsteps in the fallen leaves.

Jimmy, being as quiet as he could, made his way through the underbrush till he came round under the bridge. A stone plunked into the water.

The flounce of lace danced at Polly's neck as she stood up and turned toward the sound. She saw Jimmy through the trees.

Jimmy saw the flash of white. He pointed his gun and shot.

Polly fell.

The echo of the shot reverberated through the stand of yellow birches as a circle of smoke curled upward into the trees and lost its shape.

He ran and the forest floor crunched underfoot. Then he saw—not the fine buck he thought he had shot—but Polly. He dropped his gun to the ground and fell to his knees beside her. Her white lace was spattered with blood. She looked at Jimmy. Her breathing was faint and unsteady. Horrified and shaking, he lifted her head and cradled it in his lap. A single word whispered from her sweet mouth— "Jimmer."

Jimmy rocked back and forth, hugging her head to his chest. He tasted the salt of his tears when he said, "You'll be all right, sweetheart. I swear. You'll be okay. I'll git help—the house's just over yonder, Pol . . . oh, Polly, Polly."

Jimmy lifted Polly in his arms and carried her toward the cabin, her face snuggled to his chest. Her arm drooped toward the ground and the gentian fell from her hand.

Jimmy staggered up onto the porch, kissing Polly's head and sobbing, "You're jest hurt, sweetheart, jest hurt a little, that's all. Mama'll fix ya up." It was his mama who first said that no, she wasn't hurt, she was dead. She made Jimmy lay Polly on the divan in front of the fireplace, saying, "Land sakes, boy, try to get aholt of yerself." Jewett Randall grabbed Jimmy's shoulders and turned him around and asked him how this had happened. Jimmy told him—as best he could. But it was hard. He didn't want to admit that his precious Polly was dead—that he had shot her just like he had shot that doe ten years ago. Then Jewett said, "Son, we gotta go tell Merle and Bessie Joyce about this, jest quick's we can. It's goin' be real hard on 'em. Ain't no tellin' what ol' Merle's like to do." Jimmy nodded in agreement. Then Jewett turned to Lester and told him to go get the truck and drive over to the Vaughn place and fetch Merle. Doing as he was told, Lester stopped by the front door, put on his coat and hat, and picked up his gun. Jewett warned him to be careful.

A little later Lester's truck skidded to a stop back in front of the Randall cabin. Doors opened and slammed. Lester and Merle came rushing up onto the porch. Merle bolted through the door and when he saw Polly, he stiffened—straight as a poker. Merle was no stranger to death. He had seen a lot of it in the mines. Had nearly died a few times himself. Jewett and Lester could see the muscles in his cheeks flex.

Then Merle turned, slowly, and faced Jimmy, and with hate and anger trembling in his voice, he said, "You done this, didn't ya?" He drew back his hand to hit Jimmy, but Lester stepped in between them. Jimmy turned and walked out of the cabin and into the cold November dusk. His face was stained with tears and his throat was swollen shut with grief. He walked in a blur back to the Wilhoit Bridge. He found his gun where he had dropped it, and in a fit of rage he smashed it again and again against a tree, then hurled it, bent and splintered, into the creek.

Polly was buried a week later, on the very day she and Jimmy were to have been married. Reverend Carlester Devore started preaching a sermon about goodness and innocence and love. "Love is like the mawnin' an' the evenin' star," he began. He went on and on, about this and that, till a faint drizzle started up and forced him to quit— but not before reminding everyone about the fellowship pancake supper at the Nine Mile Baptist Church later that evening. Jimmy and his family were leaving the cemetery, heading over to their truck, when the sheriff, Hoyt Clepper, came up to Jimmy, put his hand on his shoulder, and said, "Son, I hate like the very dickens to have to do this, but . . . I gotta put ya under arrest for the murder of Miss Polly."

"Murder?" Jimmy protested. "Murder? Mr. Clepper, I loved her. She was my whole life. It was an accident. You must know that. An accident, a terrible accident. I thought I saw a deer. I thought she was a deer!" But Sheriff

Clepper, as he was putting handcuffs on Jimmy's wrists, said, "Son, I'm sorry. I believe ya, but old Merle Vaughn there has brought this here charge agin' ya and there ain't nothin' I can do about it. Anyway, I don't really think nothin'll come of it."

The drizzle turned to rain as Sheriff Clepper put Jimmy in the Model A and drove off down the gravel road toward the county seat.

They put Jimmy on a chain gang where he worked all day raking the courthouse lawn and fixing potholes in the roads all around Baldwin County. His family visited him when they could and brought him food—fried okra and turnip greens, johnnycake and smothered pork chops—all Jimmy's favorites, but Jimmy couldn't eat. Reverend Devore brought Jimmy a floppy little Bible and prayed with him and talked to him about salvation and forgiveness, and trusting in God. But Jimmy didn't hear. He did read the Bible some, though—after Reverend Devore left—and when he read that love bears all things and endures all things and that love never ends, he just leaned back and stared at the stains and peeling plaster on the ceiling of his cell, yearning for Polly. Polly. Oh, God, if only his mama hadn't hollered at him, if only he'd not gone back for that gun, that damned gun.

Despite the hard work of the chain gang, Jimmy couldn't sleep. He lay awake night after night, staring at the ceiling and thinking about Polly. Then, on the night before his trial, as Jimmy was lying on his cot, the stains on the ceiling began to move and to take shapes—shapes of strange animals—deer with tusks and turkeys with horns and boars with wings. And then the animals dissolved. And in their place he saw Polly—in a soft light—and he heard her voice: "Jimmer," her voice said lovingly, "don't you fret about tomorrow, sweetheart. You tell those men the truth. You tell them that it was an accident, and you tell them that you loved me. You tell them the truth, Jimmer. And remember that I love you and that I'll always love you, my dear, dear Jimmer. Our love will make everything right. I promise."

The next morning, Sheriff Clepper found Jimmy sleeping peacefully.

It was snowing outside the courthouse where Judge Harland T. Slaymaker was bringing the court to order. Harland T. Slaymaker didn't like long trials, especially during hunting season, and over the years, because of his hurried manner of dispatching cases, he had come to be known as "High Gear Harland."

The jurors were all men. Jimmy knew them and they knew Jimmy. They knew his daddy, too. And they knew the story of Jimmy's first kill, and they believed that they were stronger men than Jimmy. They believed that they were better hunters, too, and that they were incapable of such a mistake.

Polly's father was the first to take the stand.

His voice was slow and cold when he told the judge and

jury that it "warn't no accident. Yer Honner, I tell you it warn't like that boy sez. Couldn't've been. I tell ya he'uz too close to her not to 'uv seen her good. Thay'uz all crazy, them Randalls—him an' his daddy and that ugly brother of his, too. That boy done killed my little girl." Merle Vaughn's voice became a whisper when he said, finally, "Jimmy Randall murdered my Polly."

Jedediah Coover took the stand next. He started testifying and raving and pointing his cane at Jimmy before the clerk could swear him in. "Ya gotta sit down an' get swore in first, Jedediah, then ya kin speak yer piece," the judge said. Jedediah settled down and took his oath and started right in accusing the Randalls of poaching game on his property and of shooting one of his cows and two of his coon dogs. He said they killed his dog, Jojo, because "Jojo wuz a-chasin' a deer they'uz a-huntin'. A-huntin' on my own property, too, Judge." Even though Jedediah had no proof of this, the jurors believed it because they wanted to believe it.

Nobody testified on Jimmy's behalf. Bessie Joyce Vaughn wanted to speak up for him, but Merle wouldn't let her—told her to sit quiet and hold her peace. So, when it came time, Jimmy took the stand on his own behalf. He told the court that it was an accident, that though it was Polly's lace he saw, he thought it was the tail of a deer. He told them that he couldn't see Polly because of the underbrush between him and her. He admitted being careless and stupid and too anxious to please his family. And then he told the judge and the jury what Polly told him to say, being careful, though, not to say that Polly came to him in a dream. That'd be too much like a ghost story, and these men would never believe anything like that—especially Harland T. Slaymaker and Carlester Devore. Jimmy's testimony turned bright, almost happy, when he talked about Polly and how much he loved her, and when he finished he thought everything would be all right. He thought the jury believed him.

The jurors retired to the jury room to deliberate and came back ten minutes later. Reverend Carlester Devore, the foreman, was the last one back in. When the room was quiet, Judge Slaymaker asked for the verdict. Reverend Devore stood up and leaned forward against the banister of the jury box, all pious and solemn, and with an air of self-importance, pronounced, in his deepest preacher's voice, "Guilty, yer Honner. Guilty of murder."

On the word "murder," a rage of wind slammed open the courtroom doors. The framed portrait of George Washington fell off the wall and crashed to the floor. Dead leaves and curtains of snow blew down the aisle of the courtroom. Bitter wind blew bonnets off women's heads and danced them in the air for a moment, along with the papers off the judge's desk and John Austin Chambers's hairpiece. Then, just as suddenly, the doors slammed shut. The flag by the judge's sidebar, which had been blowing wildly, now fluttered for a moment and became still. In front of the jury box a single veil of snow swirled and billowed like lace in an open window. The jurors, their hair blown and their teeth chattering, looked at each other nervously. The snow wafted gracefully in the dark, chilled courtroom air. A moment later it began to change shape, taking on a form like a pale and translucent young woman.

Then a voice, cold and transparent like the air itself, said, "You judge my Jimmer wrongly. Don't forget—you taught him that hunting is a badge of manhood, you smeared his face with the blood of a doe. My death was an accident. Jimmer loves me, and I love Jimmer. Please judge him fairly."

The doors to the courtroom blew open again. Leaves and snow again filled the air as the lacy veil of snow disappeared through the open doors.

The doors slammed shut.

All was still for a while. Faces were pale. Skin was gooseflesh. Voices were quiet. Then, a low prattle started up among the jurors and among the people in the courtroom. Reverend Devore looked at his brother, Holmes R., in disbelief, and said, "There ain't no such thangs as ghosts!" Weldon Twyner, Fulton Upkins, and Dewitt Bodfish huddled together and resolved not to believe what they had just seen. The others just sat still, eyes wide open, staring straight ahead. All except for old Jedediah Coover, who clambered to his feet, exclaiming, "This here's some kinda trick! It's some kinda trick I tell ya, a trick ol' Jewett

A pale and translucent young woman

Randall cooked up to save his boy and to keep us from doin' what's right. I, fer one, ain't goin' to be turned around by no galdarned carnival trick."

"Hear, hear!" shouted Edmirl Stubblefield. Others joined in. "Hear, hear."

"Hang him," shouted John Austin Chambers, pulling himself to his feet and brandishing his cane above his head.

Judge Slaymaker picked up his gavel and brought it down sharply, again and again, shouting over the tumult, "Order! Order! Order in the court!"

The room got quiet. Old John Austin Chambers remained standing, his toothless mouth pouting and sucking, his eyes darting from one face to another, looking for approval. "Sit down, John Austin," Judge Slaymaker said indulgently, taking his spectacles off his nose. John Austin sat down, slowly. The judge looked at the jury. Some of them sat as still as could be, some stared at their folded hands, some fidgeted, and some crossed their arms across their chests and looked smug. A few moments passed in silence. Then Judge Slaymaker put his glasses back on his nose and appeared to be studying the scattered papers left on his desk. Finally he looked sternly over his spectacles and said, "The jury has spoken." He was quiet for a moment, then continued, "I sentence you to be hanged by the neck until you are dead."

A hush fell across the room. Eulalia Randall burst into tears. Lester and Jewett consoled her. "Sentence to be carried out one week from today at ten o'clock in the morning." He hammered down the gavel sharply, pushed his chair back from his desk, and walked briskly to his chambers.

The Randalls went home. Lester took the truck and drove off. Eulalia put on her apron, thinking she'd make some johnnycake, but she just leaned against the sink and stared out the window at the snow turning to rain. Jewett sat by the fire and cleaned his gun. When he finished, he hung it over the mantelpiece and never took it down again.

The next week Jimmy was set astride a horse and led to an old catalpa tree on the outskirts of town. A small crowd had gathered, mostly men. Some curious children were there, too, all bundled up, running around, squealing, and hiding behind wagons and trees, hoping nobody would see them and run them away. A few speckled chickens squawked and clucked alongside the road, pecking at each other and at specks in the snow. A pair of old hound dogs had run a squirrel up the tree and were dancing on their hind legs, barking at it. Old John Austin Chambers had pushed his way to the front of the gathering, whipping people aside with his cane. Reverend Devore stood next to him with his eyes closed and his head bowed, caressing his Bible. Judge Slaymaker stood in front dressed in black. Jimmy wore only a light jacket and was shivering from the cold and fear. A gentle wind blew snow in drifts and into delicate eddies. Sheriff Clepper stood on the back of his

Model A and looped the noose around Jimmy's neck. It was heavy and rough.

Then, without warning, the wind gusted and howled. The old catalpa swayed and moaned. Snow blew up from the ground in sheets and whirlwinds. And later, when the story was told, some said that just as the sheriff slapped the horse on her flank, the snow swirled about Jimmy and embraced him like a shroud of cold, white lace.

The Music of Erich Zann

H. P. LOVECRAFT

I HAVE EXAMINED MAPS of the city with the greatest care, yet have never again found the Rue d'Auseil. These maps have not been modern maps alone, for I know that names change. I have, on the contrary, delved deeply into all the antiquities of the place, and have personally explored every region, of whatever name, which could possibly answer to the street I knew as the Rue d'Auseil. But despite all I have done, it remains a humiliating fact that I cannot find the house, the street, or even the locality, where, during the last months of my impoverished life as a student of metaphysics at the university, I heard the music of Erich Zann.

That my memory is broken, I do not wonder, for my health, physical and mental, was gravely disturbed throughout the period of my residence in the Rue d'Auseil, and I recall that I took none of my few acquaintances there. But that I cannot find the place again is both singular and perplexing; for it was within a half-hour's walk of the university and was distinguished by peculiarities which could hardly be forgotten by anyone who had been there. I have never met a person who has seen the Rue d'Auseil.

The Rue d'Auseil lay across a dark river bordered by precipitous brick blear-windowed warehouses and spanned by a ponderous bridge of dark stone. It was always shadowy along that river, as if the smoke of neighboring factories shut out the sun perpetually. The river was also odorous with evil stenches which I have never smelled elsewhere, and which may someday help me to find it, since I should recognize them at once. Beyond that bridge were narrow cobbled streets with rails; and then came the ascent, at first gradual, but incredibly steep as the Rue d'Auseil was reached.

I have never seen another street as narrow and steep as the Rue d'Auseil. It was almost a cliff, closed to vehicles, consisting in several places of flights of steps, and ending at the top in a lofty ivied wall. Its paving was irregular, sometimes stone slabs, sometimes cobblestones, and sometimes bare earth with struggling greenish-gray vegetation. The houses were tall, peaked-roofed, incredibly old, and crazily leaning backward, forward, and sidewise. Occasionally an opposite pair, both leaning forward, almost met across the street like an arch; and certainly they kept most of the light from the ground below. There were a few overhead bridges from house to house across the street.

The inhabitants of that street impressed me peculiarly. At

first I thought it was because they were all silent and reticent; but later decided it was because they were all very old. I do not know how I came to live on such a street, but I was not myself when I moved there. I had been living in many poor places, always evicted for want of money; until at last I came upon that tottering house in the Rue d'Auseil kept by the paralytic Blandot. It was the third house from the top of the street, and by far the tallest of them all.

My room was on the fifth story; the only inhabited room there, since the house was almost empty. On the night I arrived I heard strange music from the peaked garret overhead, and the next day asked old Blandot about it. He told me it was an old German viol player, a strange dumb man who signed his name as Erich Zann, and who played evenings in a cheap theater orchestra; adding that Zann's desire to play in the night after his return from the theater was the reason he had chosen this lofty and isolated garret room, whose single gable window was the only point on the street from which one could look over the terminating wall at the declivity and panorama beyond.

Thereafter I heard Zann every night and although he kept me awake, I was haunted by the weirdness of his music. Knowing little of the art myself, I was yet certain that none of his harmonies had any relation to music I had heard before; and concluded that he was a composer of highly original genius. The longer I listened, the more I was fascinated, until after a week I resolved to make the old man's acquaintance.

One night as he was returning from his work, I intercepted Zann in the hallway and told him that I would like to know him and be with him when he played. He was a small, lean, bent person with shabby clothes, blue eyes, grotesque, satyrlike face, and nearly bald head; and at my first words seemed both frightened and angered. My obvious friendliness, however, finally melted him; and he grudgingly motioned me to follow him up the dark, creaking, and rickety attic stairs. His room, one of only two in the steeply pitched garret, was on the west side, toward the high wall that formed the upper end of the street. Its size was very great, and seemed the greater because of its extraordinary barrenness and neglect. Of furniture there was only a narrow iron bedstead, a dingy washstand, a small table, a large bookcase, an iron music rack, and three old-fashioned chairs. Sheets of music were piled up in disorder about the floor. The walls were of bare boards, and had probably never known plaster; whilst the abundance of dust and cobwebs made the place seem more deserted than inhabited. Evidently Erich Zann's world of beauty lay in some far cosmos of imagination.

Motioning me to sit down, the dumb man closed the door, turned the large wooden bolt, and lighted a candle to augment the one he had brought with him. He now removed his viol from its moth-eaten covering and taking it, seated himself in the least uncomfortable of the three chairs. He did not employ the music rack, but, offering no choice and playing from memory, enchanted me for over

an hour with strains I had never heard before; strains
which must have been of his own devising. To describe
their exact nature is impossible for one unversed in music.
They were a kind of fugue, with recurrent passages of the
most captivating quality, but to me they were notable for
the absence of any of the weird notes I had overheard from
my room below on other occasions.

These haunting notes I had remembered and had often
hummed and whistled inaccurately to myself, so when the
player at length laid down his bow I asked him if he would
render some of them. As I began my request the wrinkled
satyrlike face lost the bored placidity it had possessed during the playing, and seemed to show some curious mixture
of anger and fright which I had noticed when first I
accosted the old man. For a moment I was inclined to use
persuasion, regarding rather lightly the whims of senility;
and even tried to awaken my host's weirder mood by
whistling a few of the strains to which I had listened the
night before. But I did not pursue this course for more
than a moment; when the dumb musician recognized the
whistled air his face grew suddenly distorted with an
expression wholly beyond analysis, and his long, cold,
bony right hand reached out to stop my mouth and silence
the crude imitation. As he did this he further demon-
strated his eccentricity by casting a startled glance toward
the lone curtained window, as if fearful of some intruder—
a glance doubly absurd, since the garret stood high and

inaccessible above the adjacent roofs, this window being the only point on the steep street, as the concierge had told me, from which one could see over the wall at the summit.

The old man's glance brought Blandot's remark to my mind, and with a certain capriciousness I felt a wish to look out over the wide and dizzying panorama of moonlit roofs and city lights beyond the hilltop, which of all the dwelling in the Rue d'Auseil only this crabbed musician could see. I moved toward the window and would have drawn aside the nondescript curtains, when with a frightened rage even greater than before, the dumb lodger was upon me again; this time motioning with his head toward the door as he nervously strove to drag me thither with both hands. Now thoroughly disgusted with my host, I ordered him to release me, and told him I would go at once. His clutch relaxed, and as he saw my disgust and offense, his own anger seemed to subside. He tightened his relaxing grip, but this time in a friendly manner, forcing me into a chair; then with an appearance of wistfulness crossed to the lit-tered table, where he wrote many words with a pencil, in the labored French of a foreigner.

The note which he finally handed me was an appeal for tolerance and forgiveness. Zann said that he was old, lonely, and afflicted with strange fears and nervous disorders connected with his music and other things. He had enjoyed my listening to his music, and wished I would come again and not mind his eccentricities. But he could not play to another his weird harmonies, and could not bear hearing them from another; nor could he bear having anything in his room touched by another. He had not known until our hallway conversation that I could over-hear his playing in my room, and now asked me if I would arrange with Blandot to take a lower floor where I could not hear him in the night. He could, he wrote, defray the difference in rent.

As I sat deciphering the execrable French, I felt more lenient toward the old man. He was a victim of physical and nervous suffering, as was I; and my metaphysical stud-ies had taught me kindness. In the silence there came a slight sound from the window—the shutter must have rat-tled in the night wind, and for some reason I started almost as violently as did Erich Zann. So when I had finished reading, I shook my host by the hand, and departed as a friend.

The next day Blandot gave me a more expensive room on the third floor, between the apartments of an aged moneylender and the room of a respectable upholsterer. There was no one on the fourth floor.

It was not long before I found that Zann's eagerness for my company was not as great as it had seemed while he was persuading me to move down from the fifth story. He did not ask me to call on him, and when I did call he appeared uneasy and played listlessly. This was always at night—in the day he slept and would admit no one. My liking for him did not grow though the attic room and the weird music seemed to hold an odd fascination for me. I had a curious desire to look out that window, over the wall and down the unseen slope at the glittering roofs and spires which must lie outspread there. Once I went up to the garret during theater hours, when Zann was away, but the door was locked.

What I did succeed in doing was to overhear the nocturnal playing of the dumb old man. At first I would tiptoe to my old fifth floor, then I grew bold enough to climb the last creaking staircase to the peaked garret. There in the narrow hall outside the bolted door with the covered keyhole, I often heard sounds which filled me with an indefinable dread—the dread of vague wonder and brooding mystery. It was not that the sounds were hideous, for they were not; but that they held vibrations suggesting nothing on this globe or earth, and that at certain intervals they assumed a symphonic quality which I could hardly conceive as produced by one player. Certainly, Erich Zann was a genius of wild power. As the weeks passed, the playing grew wilder, whilst the old musician acquired an increasing haggardness and furtiveness pitiful to behold. He now refused to admit me at any time, and shunned me whenever we met on the stairs.

Then one night as I listened at the door, I heard the shrieking viol swell into a chaotic babel of sound; a pandemonium which would have led me to doubt my own san-

ity had there not come from behind that barred portal a
piteous proof that the horror was real—the awful, inartic-
ulate cry which only a mute can utter, and which rises only
in moments of the most terrible fear or anguish. I knocked
repeatedly at the door, but received no response.
Afterwards I waited in the black hallway, shivering with
cold and fear, till I heard the poor musician's feeble effort
to rise from the floor by the aid of a chair. Believing him
just conscious after a fainting fit, I renewed my rapping, at
the same time calling out my name reassuringly. I heard
Zann stumble to the window and close both shutter and
sash, then stumble to the door, which he falteringly
unfastened to admit me. This time his delight at having
me present was real; for his distorted face gleamed with
relief while he clutched at my coat as a child clutches at its
mother's skirts.

Shaking pathetically, the old man forced me into a chair
whilst he sank into another, beside which his viol and bow
lay carelessly on the floor. He sat for some time inactive,
nodding oddly, but having a paradoxical suggestion of
intense and frightened listening. Subsequently he seemed
to be satisfied, and crossing to a chair by the table he wrote
me a brief note, handed it to me, and returned to the table
where he began to write rapidly and incessantly. The note
implored me in the name of mercy and for the sake of my
own curiosity, to wait where I was until he prepared a full
account in German of all the marvels and terrors which

beset him. I waited and the dumb man's pencil flew.

It was perhaps an hour later, while I still waited and while the old musician's feverishly written sheets still continued to pile up, that I saw Zann start from the hint of a horrible shock. Unmistakably he was looking at the curtained window and listening shudderingly. Then I half fancied I heard a sound myself; though it was not a horrible sound, but rather an exquisitely low and infinitely distant musical note, suggesting a player in one of the neighboring houses, or in some abode beyond the lofty wall over which I had never been able to look. Upon Zann the effect was terrible, for, dropping his pencil, suddenly he rose, seized his viol, and commenced to rend the night with the wildest playing I had ever heard from his bow save when listening at the barred door.

It would be useless to describe the playing of Erich Zann on that dreadful night. It was more horrible than anything I had ever overheard, because I could now see the expression of his face and could realize that this time the motive was stark fear. He was trying to make a noise; to ward off something or drown something out—what, I could not imagine, awesome though I felt it must be. The playing grew fantastic, delirious, and hysterical, yet kept to the last the qualities of supreme genius which I knew this strange old man possessed. I recognized the air—it was a wild Hungarian dance popular in the theaters, and I reflected for a moment that this was the first time I had ever heard Zann play the work of another composer.

Louder and louder, wilder and wilder, mounted the shrieking and whining of that desperate viol. The player was dripping with an uncanny perspiration and twisted like a monkey, always looking frantically at the curtained window. In his frenzied strains I could almost see shadowy satyrs and bacchanals dancing and whirling insanely through seething abysses of clouds and smoke and lightning. And then I thought I heard a shriller, steadier note that was not from the viol; a calm deliberate, purposeful, mocking note from far away in the West.

At this juncture the shutter began to rattle in a howling night wind which had sprung up outside as if in answer to the mad playing within. Zann's screaming viol now outdid itself, emitting sounds I never thought a viol could emit. The shutter rattled more loudly, unfastened, and commenced slamming against the window. Then the glass broke shiveringly under the persistent impacts, and the chill wind rushed in, making the candles sputter and rustling the sheets of paper on the table where Zann had begun to write out his horrible secret. I looked at Zann, and saw that he was past conscious observation. His blue eyes were bulging, glassy, and sightless, and the frantic playing had become a blind, mechanical, unrecognizable orgy that no pen could even suggest.

A sudden gust, stronger than the others, caught up the manuscript and bore it toward the window. I followed the

Stark fear

flying sheets in desperation, but they were gone before I reached the demolished panes. Then I remembered my old wish to gaze from this window, the only window in the Rue d'Auseil from which one might see the slope beyond the wall, and the city outspread beneath. It was very dark, but the city's lights always burned, and I expected to see them there amidst the rain and wind. Yet, when I looked from that highest of all gable windows, looked while the candles sputtered and the insane viol howled with the night wind, I saw no city spread below, and no friendly lights gleamed from remembered streets, but only blackness of space illimitable; unimagined space much alive with motion and music, and having no semblance of anything on earth. And as I stood there looking in terror, the wind blew out both the candles in the ancient peaked garret, leaving us in savage and impenetrable darkness with chaos and pandemonium before me, and the demon madness of that night-baying viol behind me.

I staggered back in the dark, without the means of striking a light, crashing against the table, overturning a chair, and finally groped my way to the place where the blackness screamed with shocking music. To save myself and Erich Zann I could at least try, whatever the powers opposed to me. Once I thought some chill thing brushed me, and I screamed, but my scream could not be heard above that hideous viol. Suddenly out of the blackness the madly sawing bow struck me, and I knew I was close to the player. I felt ahead, touched the back of Zann's chair, and then found and shook his shoulders in an effort to bring him to his senses.

He did not respond, and still the viol shrieked on without slackening. I moved my hand to his head, whose mechanical nodding I was able to stop, and shouted in his ear that we both flee from the unknown thing of the night. But he neither answered me nor abated the frenzy of his unutterable music, while all through the garret strange currents of wind seemed to dance in the darkness and babel. When my hand touched his ear I shuddered, though I knew not why—knew not why till I felt of the still face; the ice-cold, stiffened, unbreathing face whose glossy eyes bulged uselessly into the void. And then, by some miracle, finding the door and the large, wooden bolt, I plunged wildly away from that glassy-eyed thing in the dark, and from the ghoulish howling of that accursed viol whose fury increased even as I plunged.

Leaping, floating, flying down those endless stairs through the dark house, racing mindlessly out into the narrow, steep, and ancient street of steps and tottering houses; clattering down steps and over cobbles to the lower streets and the putrid canyon-walled river; panting across the great dark bridge to the broader, healthier streets and boulevards we know; all these are terrible impressions that linger with me. And I recall that there was no wind and that the moon was out and that the lights of the city twinkled.

Despite my most careful searches and investigations, I have never since been able to find the Rue d'Auseil. But I am not wholly sorry; either for this or for the loss in undreamable abysses of the closely written sheets which alone could have explained the music of Erich Zann.

The Judge's House

BRAM STOKER

WHEN THE TIME FOR HIS EXAMINATION drew near
Malcolm Malcolmson made up his mind to go somewhere
to read by himself. He feared the attractions of the seaside,
and also he feared completely rural isolation, for of old he
knew its charms, and so he determined to find some unpre-
tentious little town where there would be nothing to dis-
tract him. He refrained from asking suggestions from any
of his friends, for he argued that each would recommend
some place of which he had knowledge, and where he had
already acquaintances. As Malcolmson wished to avoid
friends he had no wish to encumber himself with the attention of friends' friends, and so he determined to look out
for a place for himself. He packed a portmanteau with
some clothes and all the books he required, and then took
ticket for the first name on the local timetable which he did
not know.

When at the end of three hours' journey he alighted at

Benchurch, he felt satisfied that he had so far obliterated his tracks as to be sure of having a peaceful opportunity of pursuing his studies. He went straight to the one inn which the sleepy little place contained, and put up for the night. Benchurch was a market town, and once in three weeks was crowded to excess, but for the remainder of the twenty-one days it was as attractive as a desert. Malcolmson looked around the day after his arrival to try to find quarters more isolated than even so quiet an inn as "The Good Traveller" afforded. There was only one place which took his fancy, and it certainly satisfied his wildest ideas regarding quiet; in fact, quiet was not the proper word to apply to it—desolation was the only term conveying any suitable idea of its isolation. It was an old rambling, heavy-built house of the Jacobean style, with heavy gables and windows, unusually small, and set higher than was customary in such houses, and was surrounded with a high brick wall massively built. Indeed, on examination, it looked more like a fortified house than an ordinary dwelling. But all these things pleased Malcolmson. "Here," he thought, "is the very spot I have been looking for, and if I can only get opportunity of using it I shall be happy." His joy was increased when he realized beyond doubt that it was not at present inhabited.

From the post office he got the name of the agent, who was rarely surprised at the application to rent a part of the old house. Mr. Carnford, the local lawyer and agent, was a genial old gentleman, and frankly confessed his delight at anyone being willing to live in the house.

"To tell you the truth," said he, "I should be only too happy, on behalf of the owners, to let anyone have the house rent free for a term of years if only to accustom the people here to see it inhabited. It has been so long empty that some kind of absurd prejudice has grown up about it, and this can be best put down by its occupation—if only," he added with a sly glance at Malcolmson, "by a scholar like yourself, who wants it quiet for a time."

Malcolmson thought it needless to ask the agent about the "absurd prejudice"; he knew he would get more information, if he should require it, on that subject from other quarters. He paid his three months' rent, got a receipt, and the name of an old woman who would probably undertake to "do" for him, and came away with the keys in his pocket. He then went to the landlady of the inn, who was a cheerful and most kindly person, and asked her advice as to such stores and provisions as he would be likely to require. She threw up her hands in amazement when he told her where he was going to settle himself.

"Not in the Judge's House!" she said, and grew pale as she spoke. He explained the locality of the house, saying that he did no know its name. When he had finished she answered:

"Aye, sure enough—sure enough the very place! It is the Judge's House sure enough." He asked her to tell him about the place, why so called, and what there was against it. She told him that it was so called locally because it had been many years before—how long she could not say, as she was herself from another part of the country, but she thought it must have been a hundred years or more—the abode of a judge who was held in great terror on account of his harsh sentences and his hostility to prisoners at Assizes. As to what there was against the house itself she could not tell. She had often asked, but no one could inform her; but there was a general feeling that there was *something,* and for her own part she would not take all the money in Drinkwater's Bank and stay in the house an hour by herself. Then she apologized to Malcolmson for her disturbing talk.

"It is too bad of me, sir, and you—and a young gentleman, too—if you will pardon me saying it, going to live there all alone. If you were my boy—and you'll excuse me for saying it—you wouldn't sleep there a night, not if I had to go there myself and pull the big alarm bell that's on the roof!" The good creature was so manifestly in earnest, and was so kindly in her intentions, that Malcolmson, although amused, was touched. He told her kindly how much he appreciated her interest in him, and added:

"But, my dear Mrs. Witham, indeed you need not be concerned about me! A man who is reading for the Mathematical Tripos has too much to think of to be disturbed by any of these mysterious 'somethings,' and his work is of too exact and prosaic a kind to allow of his having any corner in his mind for mysteries of any kind. Harmonical Progression, Permutations and Combinations, and Elliptic Functions have sufficient mysteries for me!" Mrs. Witham kindly undertook to see after his commissions, and he went himself to look for the old woman who had been recommended to him. When he returned to the Judge's House with her, after an interval of a couple of hours, he found Mrs. Witham herself waiting with several men and boys carrying parcels, and an upholsterer's man with a bed in a cart, for she said, though tables and chairs might be all very well, a bed that hadn't been aired for mayhap fifty years was not proper for young bones to lie on. She was evidently curious to see the inside of the house; and though manifestly so afraid of the "something" that at the slightest sound she clutched on to Malcolmson, whom she never left for a moment, went over the whole place.

After his examination of the house, Malcolmson decided to take up his abode in the great dining room, which was big enough to serve for all his requirements; and Mrs. Witham, with the aid of the charwoman, Mrs. Dempster, proceeded to arrange matters. When the hampers were brought in and unpacked, Malcolmson saw that with much kind forethought she had sent from her own kitchen sufficient provisions to last for a few days. Before going she expressed all sorts of kind wishes; and at the door turned and said:

"And perhaps, sir, as the room is big and drafty it might be well to have one of those big screens put round your bed at night—though, truth to tell, I would die myself if I were to be so shut in with all kinds of—of 'things,' that put their heads round the sides, or over the top, and look on me!" The image which she had called up was too much for her nerves, and she fled incontinently.

Mrs. Dempster sniffed in a superior manner as the landlady disappeared, and remarked that for her own part she wasn't afraid of all the bogies in the kingdom.

"I'll tell you what it is, sir," she said; "bogies is all kinds and sorts of things—except bogies! Rats and mice, and beetles; and creaky doors, and loose slates, and broken panes, and stiff drawer handles, that stay out when you pull them and then fall down in the middle of the night. Look at the wainscot of the room! It is old—hundreds of years old! Do you think there's no rats and beetles there! And do you imagine, sir, that you won't see none of them! Rats is bogies, I tell you, and bogies is rats; and don't you get to think anything else!"

"Mrs. Dempster," said Malcolmson gravely, making her a polite bow, "you know more than a Senior Wrangler! And let me say that, as a mark of esteem for your indubitable soundness of head and heart, I shall, when I go, give you possession of this house, and let you stay here by yourself for the last two months of my tenancy, for four weeks will serve my purpose."

"Thank you kindly, sir!" she answered. "But I couldn't

sleep away from home a night. I am in Greenhow's Charity, and if I slept a night away from my rooms I should lose all I have got to live on. The rules is very strict; and there's too many watching for a vacancy for me to run any risks in the matter. Only for that, sir, I'd gladly come here and attend on you altogether during your stay."

"My good woman," said Malcolmson hastily, "I have come here on purpose to obtain solitude; and believe me that I am grateful to the late Greenhow for having so organized his admirable charity—whatever it is—that I am perforce denied the opportunity of suffering from such a form of temptation! Saint Anthony himself could not be more rigid on the point!"

The old woman laughed harshly. "Ah, you young gentlemen," she said, "you don't fear for naught; and belike you'll get all the solitude you want here." She set to work with her cleaning; and by nightfall, when Malcolmson returned from his walk—he always had one of his books to study as he walked—he found the room swept and tidied, a fire burning in the old hearth, the lamp lit, and the table spread for supper with Mrs. Witham's excellent fare. "This is comfort, indeed," he said, as he rubbed his hands.

When he had finished his supper, and lifted the tray to the other end of the great oak dining table, he got out his books again, put fresh wood on the fire, trimmed his lamp, and set himself down to a spell of real hard work. He went on without pause till about eleven o'clock, when he knocked off for a bit to fix his fire and lamp, and to make himself a cup of tea. He had always been a tea drinker, and during his college life had sat late at work and had taken tea late. The rest was a great luxury to him, and he enjoyed it with a sense of delicious, voluptuous ease. The renewed fire leaped and sparkled, and threw quaint shadows through the great old room; and as he sipped his hot tea he reveled in the sense of isolation from his kind. Then it was that he began to notice for the first time what a noise the rats were making.

"Surely," he thought, "they cannot have been at it all the time I was reading. Had they been, I must have noticed it!" Presently, when the noise increased, he satisfied himself that it was really new. It was evident that at first the rats had been frightened at the presence of a stranger, and the light of fire and lamp; but that as the time went on they had grown bolder and were now disporting themselves as was their wont.

How busy they were! And hark to the strange noises! Up and down behind the old wainscot, over the ceiling and under the floor they raced, and gnawed, and scratched! Malcolmson smiled to himself as he recalled to mind the saying of Mrs. Dempster, "Bogies is rats, and rats is bogies!" The tea began to have its effect of intellectual and nervous stimulus; he saw with joy another long spell of work to be done before the night was past, and in the sense of security which it gave him, he allowed himself the luxury of a good look round the room. He took his lamp in one hand, and went all around, wondering that so quaint and beautiful an old house had been so long neglected. The carving of the oak on the panels of the wainscot was fine, and on and round the doors and windows it was beautiful and of rare merit. There were some old pictures on the walls, but they were coated so thick with dust and dirt that he could not distinguish any detail of them, though he held his lamp as high as he could over his head. Here and there as he went round he saw some crack or hole blocked for a moment by the face of a rat with its bright eyes glittering in the light, but in an instant it was gone, and a squeak and a scamper followed.

The thing that most struck him, however, was the rope of the great alarm bell on the roof, which hung down in a corner of the room on the right-hand side of the fireplace. He pulled up close to the hearth a great high-backed carved oak chair, and sat down to his last cup of tea. When this was done he made up the fire, and went back to his work, sitting at the corner of the table, having the fire to his left. For a while the rats disturbed him somewhat with their perpetual scampering, but he got accustomed to the noise as one does to the ticking of a clock or to the roar of moving water; and he became so immersed in his work that everything in the world, except the problem which he was trying to solve, passed away from him.

He suddenly looked up; his problem was still unsolved,

and there was in the air that sense of the hour before the dawn, which is so dread to doubtful life. The noise of the rats had ceased. Indeed it seemed to him that it must have ceased but lately and that it was the sudden cessation which had disturbed him. The fire had fallen low, but still it threw out a deep red glow. As he looked he started in spite of his *sangfroid*.

There on the great high-backed carved oak chair by the right side of the fireplace sat an enormous rat, steadily glaring at him with baleful eyes. He made a motion to it as though to hunt it away, but it did not stir. Then he made the motion of throwing something. Still it did not stir, but showed its great white teeth angrily, and its cruel eyes shone in the lamplight with an added vindictiveness.

Malcolmson felt amazed, and seizing the poker from the hearth ran at it to kill it. Before, however, he could strike it, the rat, with a squeak that sounded like the concentration of hate, jumped upon the floor, and, running up the rope of the alarm bell, disappeared in the darkness beyond the range of the green-shaded lamp. Instantly, strange to say, the noisy scampering of the rats in the wainscot began again.

By this time Malcolmson's mind was quite off the problem; and as a shrill cock crow outside told him of the approach of morning, he went to bed and to sleep.

He slept so sound that he was not even waked by Mrs. Dempster coming in to make up his room. It was only when she had tidied up the place and got his breakfast ready and tapped on the screen which closed in his bed that he woke. He was a little tired still after his night's hard work, but a strong cup of tea soon freshened him up, and, taking his book, he went out for his morning walk, bringing with him a few sandwiches lest he should not care to return till dinnertime. He found a quiet walk between high elms some way outside the town, and here he spent the greater part of the day studying his Laplace. On his return he looked in to see Mrs. Witham and to thank her for her kindness. When she saw him coming through the diamond-paned bay window of her sanctum she came out to meet him and asked him in. She looked at him searchingly and shook her head as she said:

"You must not overdo it, sir. You are paler this morning than you should be. Too late hours and too hard work on the brain isn't good for any man! But tell me, sir, how did you pass the night? Well, I hope? But, my heart! Sir, I was glad when Mrs. Dempster told me this morning that you were all right and sleeping sound when she went in."

"Oh, I was all right," he answered, smiling, "the 'somethings' didn't worry me, as yet. Only the rats; and they had a circus, I tell you, all over the place. There was one wicked looking old devil that sat up on my own chair by the fire, and wouldn't go till I took the poker to him, and then he ran up the rope of the alarm bell and got to somewhere up the wall or the ceiling—I couldn't see where, it was so dark."

"Mercy on us," said Mrs. Witham, "an old devil, and sitting on a chair by the fireside! Take care, sir! Take care! There's many a true word spoken in jest."

"How do you mean? 'Pon my word I don't understand."

"An old devil! The old devil, perhaps. There! Sir, you needn't laugh," for Malcolmson had broken into a hearty peal. "You young folks thinks it easy to laugh at things that makes older ones shudder. Never mind, sir! Never mind! Please God, you'll laugh all the time. It's what I wish you myself!" And the good lady beamed all over in sympathy with his enjoyment, her fears gone for a moment.

"Oh, forgive me!" said Malcolmson presently. "Don't think me rude; but the idea was too much for me—that the old devil himself was on the chair last night!" And at the thought he laughed again. Then he went home to dinner.

This evening the scampering of the rats began earlier; indeed it had been going on before his arrival, and only ceased whilst his presence by its freshness disturbed them. After dinner he sat by the fire for a while and had a smoke; and then, having cleared his table, began to work as before. Tonight the rats disturbed him more than they had done on the previous night. How they scampered up and down and under and over! How they squeaked, and scratched, and gnawed! How they, getting bolder by degrees, came to the mouths of their holes and to the chinks and cracks and crannies in the wainscoting till their eyes shone like tiny lamps as the firelight rose and fell. But to him, now doubtless accustomed to them, their eyes were not wicked; only their playfulness touched him. Sometimes the boldest of them made sallies out on the floor or along the moldings of the wainscot. Now and again as they disturbed him Malcolmson made a sound to frighten them, smiting the table with his hand or giving a fierce "Hsh, hsh," so that they fled straightway to their holes.

And so the early part of the night wore on; and despite the noise Malcolmson got more and more immersed in his work.

All at once he stopped, as on the previous night, being overcome by a sudden sense of silence. There was not the faintest sound of gnaw, or scratch, or squeak. The silence was as of the grave. He remembered the odd occurrence of the previous night, and instinctively he looked at the chair standing close by the fireside. And then a very odd sensation thrilled through him.

There, on the great old high-backed carved oak chair beside the fireplace, sat the same enormous rat, steadily glaring at him with baleful eyes.

Instinctively he took the nearest thing to his hand, a book of logarithms, and flung it at it. The book was badly aimed and the rat did not stir, so again the poker performance of the previous night was repeated; and again the rat, being closely pursued, fled up the rope of the alarm bell. Strangely too, the departure of this rat was instantly followed by the renewal of the noise made by the general rat community. On this occasion, as on the previous one, Malcolmson could not see at what part of the room the rat disappeared, for the green shade of his lamp left the upper part of the room in darkness, and the fire had burned low.

On looking at his watch he found it was close on midnight; and, not sorry for the *divertissement,* he made up his fire and made himself his nightly pot of tea. He had got through a good spell of work, and thought himself entitled to a cigarette; and so he sat on the great carved oak chair before the fire and enjoyed it. Whilst smoking he began to think that he would like to know where the rat disappeared to, for he had certain ideas for the morrow not entirely disconnected with a rattrap. Accordingly he lit another lamp and placed it so that it would shine well into the right-hand corner of the wall by the fireplace. Then he got all the books he had with him, and placed them handy to throw at the vermin. Finally he lifted the rope of the alarm bell and placed the end of it on the table, fixing the extreme end under the lamp. As he handled it he could not help noticing how pliable it was, especially for so strong a rope, and one not in use. "You could hang a man with it," he thought to himself. When his preparations were made he looked around, and said complacently:

"There now, my friend, I think we shall learn something of you this time!" He began his work again, and though as before somewhat disturbed at first by the noise of the rats, soon lost himself in his propositions and problems.

Again he was called to his immediate surroundings suddenly. This time it might not have been the sudden silence only which took his attention; there was a slight movement of the rope, and the lamp moved. Without stirring, he looked to see if his pile of books was within range, and then cast his eye along the rope. As he looked he saw the great rat drop from the rope on the oak armchair and sit there glaring at him. He raised a book in his right hand, and taking careful aim, flung it at the rat. The latter, with a quick movement, sprang aside and dodged the missile. He then took another book, and a third, and flung them one after another at the rat, but each time unsuccessfully. At last, as he stood with a book poised in his hand to throw, the rat squeaked and seemed afraid. This made Malcolmson more than ever eager to strike, and the book flew and struck the rat a resounding blow. It gave a terrified squeak, and turning on its pursuer a look of terrible malevolence, ran up the chairback and made a great jump to the rope of the alarm bell and ran up it like lightning. The lamp rocked under the sudden strain, but it was a heavy one and did not topple over. Malcolmson kept his eyes on the rat, and saw it by the light of the second lamp leap to a molding of the wainscot and disappear through a hole in one of the great pictures which hung on the wall, obscured and invisible through its coating of dirt and dust.

"I shall look up my friend's habitation in the morning," said the student, as he went over to collect his books. "The

A look of terrible malevolence

third picture from the fireplace; I shall not forget." He picked up the books one by one, commenting on them as he lifted them. "*Conic Sections* he does not mind, nor *Cycloidal Oscillations*, nor the *Principia*, nor *Quaternions*, nor *Thermodynamics*. Now for the book that fetched him!" Malcolmson took it up and looked at it. As he did so he started, and a sudden pallor overspread his face. He looked round uneasily and shivered slightly, as he murmured to himself:

"The Bible my mother gave me! What an odd coincidence." He sat down to work again, and the rats in the wainscot renewed their gambols. They did not disturb him, however; somehow their presence gave him a sense of companionship. But he could not attend to his work, and after striving to master the subject on which he was engaged gave it up in despair, and went to bed as the first streak of dawn stole in through the eastern window.

He slept heavily but uneasily, and dreamed much; and when Mrs. Dempster woke him late in the morning he seemed ill at ease, and for a few minutes did not seem to realize exactly where he was. His first request rather surprised the servant.

"Mrs. Dempster, when I am out today I wish you would get the steps and dust or wash those pictures—specially that one the third from the fireplace—I want to see what they are."

Late in the afternoon Malcolmson worked at his books

in the shaded walk, and the cheerfulness of the previous day came back to him as the day wore on, and he found that his reading was progressing well. He had worked out to a satisfactory conclusion all the problems which had as yet baffled him, and it was in a state of jubilation that he paid a visit to Mrs. Witham at "The Good Traveller." He found a stranger in the cozy sitting room with the landlady, who was introduced to him as Dr. Thornhill. She was not quite at ease, and this, combined with the Doctor's plunging at once into a series of questions, made Malcolmson come to the conclusion that his presence was not an accident, so without preliminary he said:

"Dr. Thornhill, I shall with pleasure answer you any question you may choose to ask me if you will answer me one question first."

The Doctor seemed surprised, but he smiled and answered at once. "Done! What is it?"

"Did Mrs. Witham ask you to come here and see me and advise me?"

Dr. Thornhill for a moment was taken aback, and Mrs. Witham got fiery red and turned away; but the Doctor was a frank and ready man, and he answered at once and openly:

"She did: but she didn't intend you to know it. I suppose it was my clumsy haste that made you suspect. She told me that she did not like the idea of your being in that house all by yourself, and that she thought you took too much strong tea. In fact, she wants me to advise you if possible to give up the tea and the very late hours. I was a keen student in my time, so I suppose I may take the liberty of a college man, and without offense, advise you not quite as a stranger."

Malcolmson with a bright smile held out his hand. "Shake! As they say in America," he said. "I must thank you for your kindness and Mrs. Witham too, and your kindness deserves a return on my part. I promise to take no more strong tea—no tea at all till you let me—and I shall go to bed tonight at one o'clock at latest. Will that do?"

"Capital," said the Doctor. "Now tell us all that you noticed in the old house," and so Malcolmson then and there told in minute detail all that had happened in the last two nights. He was interrupted every now and then by some exclamation from Mrs. Witham, till finally when he told of the episode of the Bible the landlady's pent-up emotions found vent in a shriek; and it was not till a stiff glass of brandy and water had been administered that she grew composed again. Dr. Thornhill listened with a face of growing gravity, and when the narrative was complete and Mrs. Witham had been restored he asked:

"The rat always went up the rope of the alarm bell?"

"Always."

"I suppose you know," said the Doctor after a pause, "what the rope is?"

"No!"

"It is," said the Doctor slowly, "the very rope which the hangman used for all the victims of the Judge's judicial rancor!" Here he was interrupted by another scream from Mrs. Witham, and steps had to be taken for her recovery. Malcolmson having looked at his watch, and found that it was close to his dinner hour, had gone home before her complete recovery.

When Mrs. Witham was herself again she almost assailed the Doctor with angry questions as to what he meant by putting such horrible ideas into the poor young man's mind. "He has quite enough there already to upset him," she added. Dr. Thornhill replied:

"My dear madam, I had a distinct purpose in it! I wanted to draw his attention to the bell rope, and to fix it there. It may be that he is in a highly overwrought state, and has been studying too much, although I am bound to say that he seems as sound and healthy a young man, mentally and bodily, as ever I saw—but then the rats—and that suggestion of the devil." The Doctor shook his head and went on. "I would have offered to go and stay the first night with him but that I felt sure it would have been a cause of offense. He may get in the night some strange fright or hallucination; and if he does I want him to pull that rope. All alone as he is it will give us warning, and we may reach him in time to be of service. I shall be sitting up pretty late tonight and shall keep my ears open. Do not be alarmed if Benchurch gets a surprise before morning."

"Oh, Doctor, what do you mean? What do you mean?"

"I mean this; that possibly—nay, more probably—we shall hear the great alarm bell from the Judge's House tonight," and the Doctor made about as effective an exit as could be thought of.

When Malcolmson arrived home he found that it was a little after his usual time, and Mrs. Dempster had gone away—the rules of Greenhow's Charity were not to be neglected. He was glad to see that the place was bright and tidy with a cheerful fire and a well-trimmed lamp. The evening was colder than might have been expected in April, and a heavy wind was blowing with such rapidly increasing strength that there was every promise of a storm during the night. For a few minutes after his entrance the noise of the rats ceased; but so soon as they became accustomed to his presence they began again. He was glad to hear them, for he felt once more the feeling of companionship in their noise, and his mind ran back to the strange fact that they only ceased to manifest themselves when that other—the great rat with the baleful eyes—came upon the scene. The reading lamp only was lit and its green shade kept the ceiling and the upper part of the room in darkness, so that the cheerful light from the hearth spreading over the floor and shining on the white cloth laid over the end of the table was warm and cheery. Malcolmson sat down to his dinner with a good appetite and a buoyant spirit. After his dinner and a cigarette he sat steadily down to work, determined not to let anything disturb him, for he remembered his promise to the Doctor, and made up his mind to make the best of the time at his disposal.

For an hour or so he worked all right, and then his thoughts began to wander from his books. The actual circumstances around him, the calls on his physical attention, and his nervous susceptibility were not to be denied. By this time the wind had become a gale, and the gale a storm. The old house, solid though it was, seemed to shake to its foundations, and the storm roared and raged through its many chimneys and its queer old gables, producing strange, unearthly sounds in the empty rooms and corridors. Even the great alarm bell on the roof must have felt the force of the wind, for the rope rose and fell slightly, as though the bell were moved a little from time to time, and the limber rope fell on the oak floor with a hard and hollow sound.

As Malcolmson listened to it he bethought himself of the Doctor's words, "It is the rope which the hangman used for the victims of the Judge's judicial rancor," and he went over to the corner of the fireplace and took it in his hand to look at it. There seemed a sort of deadly interest in it, and as he stood there he lost himself for a moment in speculation as to who these victims were, and the grim wish of the Judge to have such a ghastly relic ever under his eyes. As he stood there the swaying of the bell on the roof still lifted the rope now and again; but presently there came a new sensation—a sort of tremor in the rope, as though something was moving along it.

Looking up instinctively Malcolmson saw the great rat coming slowly down towards him, glaring at him steadily. He dropped the rope and started back with a muttered curse, and the rat turning ran up the rope again and disappeared, and at the same instant Malcolmson became conscious that the noise of the rats, which had ceased for a while, began again.

All this set him thinking, and it occurred to him that he had not investigated the lair of the rat or looked at the pictures, as he had intended. He lit the other lamp without the shade, and, holding it up, went and stood opposite the third picture from the fireplace on the right-hand side where he had seen the rat disappear on the previous night.

At the first glance he started back so suddenly that he almost dropped the lamp, and a deadly pallor overspread his face. His knees shook, and heavy drops of sweat came on his forehead, and he trembled like an aspen. But he was young and plucky, and pulled himself together, and after the pause of a few seconds stepped forward again, raised the lamp, and examined the picture which had been dusted and washed, and now stood out clearly.

It was of a judge dressed in his robes of scarlet and ermine. His face was strong and merciless, evil, crafty, and vindictive, with a sensual mouth, hooked nose of ruddy color, and shaped like the beak of a bird of prey. The rest of the face was of a cadaverous color. The eyes were of peculiar brilliance and with a terribly malignant expression. As he looked at them, Malcolmson grew cold, for he saw there the very counterpart of the eyes of the great rat. The lamp almost fell from his hand; he saw the rat with its baleful eyes peering out through the hole in the corner of the picture, and noted the sudden cessation of the noise of the other rats. However, he pulled himself together, and went on with his examination of the picture.

The Judge was seated in a great high-backed carved oak chair, on the right-hand side of a great stone fireplace where, in the corner, a rope hung down from the ceiling, its end lying coiled on the floor. With a feeling of something like horror, Malcolmson recognized the scene of the room as it stood, and gazed around him in an awestruck manner as though he expected to find some strange presence behind him. Then he looked over to the corner of the fireplace—and with a loud cry he let the lamp fall from his hand.

There, in the Judge's armchair, with the rope hanging behind, sat the rat with the Judge's baleful eyes, now intensified and with a fiendish leer. Save for the howling of the storm without there was silence.

The fallen lamp recalled Malcolmson to himself. Fortunately it was of metal, and so the oil was not spilt. However, the practical need of attending to it settled at once his nervous apprehensions. When he had turned it out, he wiped his brow and thought for a moment.

"This will not do," he said to himself. "If I go on like this I shall become a crazy fool. This must stop! I promised the Doctor I would not take tea. Faith, he was pretty right! My nerves must have been getting into a queer state. Funny I did not notice it. I never felt better in my life. However, it is all right now, and I shall not be such a fool again."

Then he mixed himself a good stiff glass of brandy and water and resolutely sat down to his work.

It was nearly an hour when he looked up from his book, disturbed by the sudden stillness. Without, the wind howled and roared louder than ever, and the rain drove in sheets against the windows, beating like hail on the glass; but within there was no sound whatever save the echo of the wind as it roared in the great chimney, and now and then a hiss as a few raindrops found their way down the chimney in a lull of the storm. The fire had fallen low and had ceased to flame, though it threw out a red glow. Malcolmson listened attentively, and presently heard a thin, squeaking noise, very faint. It came from the corner of the room where the rope hung down, and he thought it was the creaking of the rope on the floor as the swaying of the bell raised and lowered it. Looking up, however, he saw in the dim light the great rat clinging to the rope and gnawing it. The rope was already nearly gnawed through—he could see the lighter color where the strands were laid bare. As he looked the job was completed, and the severed end of the rope fell clattering on the oaken floor, whilst for an instant the great rat remained like a knob or tassel at the end of the rope, which now began to sway to and fro. Malcolmson felt for a moment another pang of terror as he thought that now the possibility of calling the outer world to his assistance was cut off, but an intense anger took its place, and seizing the book he was reading he hurled it at the rat. The blow was well aimed, but before the missile could reach it the rat dropped off and struck the floor with a soft thud. Malcolmson instantly rushed over towards it, but it darted away and disappeared in the darkness of the shadows of the room. Malcolmson felt that his work was over for the night, and determined then and there to vary the monotony of the proceedings by a hunt for the rat, and took off the green shade of the lamp so as to insure a wider spreading light. As he did so the gloom of the upper part of the room was relieved, and in the new flood of light, great by comparison with the previous darkness, the pictures on the wall stood out boldly. From where he stood, Malcolmson saw right opposite to him the third picture on the wall from the right of the fireplace. He rubbed his eyes in surprise, and then a great fear began to come upon him.

In the center of the picture was a great irregular patch of brown canvas, as fresh as when it was stretched on the frame. The background was as before, with chair and chimney corner and rope, but the figure of the Judge had disappeared.

Malcolmson, almost in a chill of horror, turned slowly round, and then he began to shake and tremble like a man in a palsy. His strength seemed to have left him, and he was incapable of action or movement, hardly even of thought. He could only see and hear.

There, on the great high-backed carved oak chair sat the Judge in his robes of scarlet and ermine, with his baleful eyes glaring vindictively, and a smile of triumph on the res-olute, cruel mouth, as he lifted with his hands a *black cap*. Malcolmson felt as if the blood was running from his heart, as one does in moments of prolonged suspense. There was a singing in his ears. Without, he could hear the roar and howl of the tempest, and through it, swept on the storm, came the striking of midnight by the great chimes in the market place. He stood for a space of time that seemed to him endless, still as a statue and with wide-open, horror-struck eyes, breathless. As the clock struck, so the smile of triumph on the Judge's face intensified, and at the last stroke of midnight he placed the black cap on his head.

Slowly and deliberately the Judge rose from his chair and picked up the piece of rope of the alarm bell which lay on the floor, drew it through his hands as if he enjoyed its touch, and then deliberately began to knot one end of it, fashioning it into a noose. This he tightened and tested with his foot, pulling hard at it till he was satisfied and then making a running noose of it, which he held in his hand. Then he began to move along the table on the opposite side to Malcolmson, keeping his eyes on him until he had passed him, when with a quick movement he stood in front of the door. Malcolmson then began to feel that he was trapped, and tried to think of what he should do. There was some fascination in the Judge's eyes, which he never took off him, and he had, perforce, to look. He saw the Judge approach—still keeping between him and the door—and raise the noose and throw it towards him as if to entangle him. With a great effort he made a quick movement to one side, and saw the rope fall beside him, and heard it strike the oaken floor. Again the Judge raised the noose and tried to ensnare him, ever keeping his baleful eyes fixed on him, and each time by a mighty effort the student just managed to evade it. So this went on for many times, the Judge seeming never discouraged nor discomposed at failure, but playing as a cat does with a mouse. At last in despair, which had reached its climax, Malcolmson cast a quick glance round him. The lamp seemed to have blazed up, and there was a fairly good light in the room. At the many ratholes and in the chinks and crannies of the wainscot he saw the rats' eyes; and this aspect, that was purely physical, gave him a gleam of comfort. He looked around and saw that the rope of the great alarm bell was laden with rats. Every inch of it was covered with them, and more and more were pouring through the small circular hole in the ceiling whence it emerged, so that with their weight the bell was beginning to sway.

Hark! It had swayed till the clapper had touched the bell.

The sound was but a tiny one, but the bell was only beginning to sway, and it would increase.

At the sound the Judge, who had been keeping his eyes fixed on Malcolmson, looked up, and a scowl of diabolical anger overspread his face. His eyes fairly glowed like hot coals, and he stamped his foot with a sound that seemed to make the house shake. A dreadful peal of thunder broke overhead as he raised the rope again, whilst the rats kept running up and down the rope as though working against time. This time, instead of throwing it, he drew close to his victim, and held open the noose as he approached. As he came closer there seemed something paralyzing in his very presence, and Malcolmson stood rigid as a corpse. He felt the Judge's icy fingers touch his throat as he adjusted the rope. The noose tightened—tightened. Then the Judge, taking the rigid form of the student in his arms, carried him over and placed him standing in the oak chair, and stepping up beside him, put his hand up and caught the end of the swaying rope of the alarm bell. As he raised his hand the rats fled squeaking, and disappeared through the hole in the ceiling. Taking the end of the noose which was round Malcolmson's neck he tied it to the hanging bell rope, and then descending pulled away the chair.

When the alarm bell of the Judge's House began to sound a crowd soon assembled. Lights and torches of various kinds appeared, and soon a silent crowd was hurrying to the spot. They knocked loudly at the door, but there was no reply. Then they burst in the door, and poured into the great dining room, the Doctor at the head.

There at the end of the rope of the great alarm bell hung the body of the student, and on the face of the Judge in the picture was a malignant smile.

Dead Aaron

RETOLD BY JAMES HASKINS

AARON KELLY DIED, so they buried him. That night the mourners were sitting around the fire.

His widow was saying, "I hope he's gone, but I suspect he isn't," when in walked the corpse.

The corpse sat down between the widow and the lead mourner and said, "What's this all about? You all act like somebody's dead. Who's dead?"

"You are," said the widow, shaking like a leaf.

"Me dead?" said Aaron Kelly. "How come? I don't feel dead."

The others told him, "You don't feel dead, but you look dead, Aaron. You better go back to the grave where you belong."

"No," said Aaron. "I'm not going back to any grave until I feel dead." With that, he moved closer to the fire and started trying to warm his hands and feet, all the while giving a chill to the room that hadn't been there before. That's all he did, night and day, was sit by the fire.

Well, that sure presented a problem. For one thing, Aaron Kelly sure looked dead. His joints cracked, his skin looked dusty. His widow and the other mourners weren't sure how long the corpse was going to last. But that was just part of the problem. The insurance association wouldn't pay on his life insurance policy because Aaron swore he wasn't dead. And the undertaker said he was going to take back the coffin if Aaron wasn't going to occupy it.

Aaron's widow tried to explain all this to Aaron, but he wouldn't listen. "Let me be, woman!" he said. "I'm not going back to any burying ground until I'm dead. Don't you miss me?"

"Miss you?" she wanted to know. "How am I going to miss you? I haven't had a chance to miss you. You're not gone."

"Aren't you going to mourn for me?" Aaron next wanted to know.

She replied, "What's the use of going into mourning when I haven't lost you yet?"

"You haven't paid proper attention to me," he charged.

"Haven't paid proper attention?" she wanted to know. "Didn't we take you out and bury you? Didn't the Reverend preach the funeral? You think we're going to bury you two times? Well, we aren't. So quit complaining."

Aaron just sat by the fire and creaked and cracked. His joints were dry, his back was stiff, and every time he

How that dead man could dance!

moved, he cracked and creaked like a dead tree in the wind.

One night the best fiddler in town came to court the widow. He sat on one side of the fire, and Aaron sat on the other, trying to warm his hands and feet and creaking and cracking. The fiddler grew tired of hearing Aaron creak and crack. The widow was tired of the whole situation.

"How long do we have to put up with this dead corpse?" she wanted to know. "How long do we have to wait until he molders? How long do we have to sit by our own fire, you, and me, and *him*?"

But the fiddler didn't have any answers.

By and by Aaron Kelly rose and stretched and said, "This isn't much fun. Let's have some fun. Let's dance to limber up our legs."

So the fiddler got out his fiddle and began to play, and Aaron got up to dance. He shook himself. He took a step or two. He began to do a jig, with his old bones cracking and his yellow teeth snapping, his knee bones knocking, and his arms flip-flopping, around and around and around. He skipped and he pranced, and how that dead man could dance!

Pretty soon a piece of him flew loose and fell to the floor.

"My golly, look at that!" said the fiddler.

"Play faster!" cried the widow.

The fiddler played faster. Dead Aaron danced faster, and pieces of bone kept popping and dropping every which way. With every hop a dry bone dropped.

"Oh, my God!" cried the fiddler.

"Play, man, play!" hollered the widow.

The fiddler played faster. Dead Aaron danced faster, bones dropping all around, until all at once he crumbled down, and there Dead Aaron lay, just a heap of bones on the floor, except for the bald head, which danced by itself, grinning at the fiddler.

"Play faster yet!" cried the widow. But the fiddler wasn't interested in playing for a grinning, dancing skull.

"Widow, I've got to go get me some more rosin for my bow," he said, and he took off running.

They gathered the bones together and put them back in the grave. But they were careful to lay the bones one across the other and all confused, so Aaron couldn't figure out how they went back together. After that, Dead Aaron didn't get up out of the grave anymore.

The widow remained a widow from that day on, though. That dancing head spoiled her chances for romance.

The Ghost Ship
RICHARD MIDDLETON

FAIRFIELD IS A LITTLE VILLAGE LYING NEAR the Portsmouth Road about halfway between London and the sea. Strangers who find it by accident now and then call it a pretty, old-fashioned place; we who live in it and call it home don't find anything very pretty about it, but we should be sorry to live anywhere else. Our minds have taken the shape of the inn and the church and the green, I suppose. At all events, we never feel comfortable out of Fairfield.

Of course the Cockneys, with their vasty houses and noise-ridden streets, can call us rustics if they choose, but for all that Fairfield is a better place to live in than London. Doctor says that when he goes to London his mind is bruised with the weight of the houses, and he was a Cockney born. He had to live there himself when he was a little chap, but he knows better now. You gentlemen may laugh—perhaps some of you come from London way—

but it seems to me that a witness like that is worth a gallon of arguments.

Dull? Well, you might find it dull, but I assure you that I've listened to all the London yarns you have spun to-night, and they're absolutely nothing to the things that happen at Fairfield. It's because of our way of thinking and minding our own business. If one of your Londoners were set down on the green of a Saturday night when the ghosts of the lads who died in the war keep tryst with the lasses who lie in the churchyard, he couldn't help being curious and interfering, and then the ghosts would go somewhere where it was quieter. But we just let them come and go and don't make any fuss, and in consequence Fairfield is the ghostliest place in all England. Why, I've seen a headless man sitting on the edge of the well in broad daylight, and the children playing about his feet as if he were their father. Take my word for it, spirits know when they are well off as much as human beings.

Still, I must admit that the thing I'm going to tell you about was queer even for our part of the world, where three packs of ghost hounds hunt regularly during the season, and blacksmith's great-grandfather is busy all night shoeing the dead gentlemen's horses. Now that's a thing that wouldn't happen in London, because of their interfering ways, but blacksmith he lies up aloft and sleeps as quiet as a lamb. Once when he had a bad head he shouted down to them not to make so much noise, and in the morning he found an old guinea left on the anvil as an apology. He wears it on his watch chain now. But I must get on with my story; if I start telling you about the queer happenings at Fairfield I'll never stop.

It all came of the great storm in the spring of '97, the year that we had two great storms. This was the first one, and I remember it very well, because I found in the morning that it had lifted the thatch of my pigsty into the widow's garden as clean as a boy's kite. When I looked over the hedge, widow—Tom Lamport's widow that was—was prodding for her nasturtiums with a daisy grubber. After I had watched her for a little I went down to the "Fox and Grapes" to tell landlord what she had said to me. Landlord he laughed, being a married man and at ease with the sex. "Come to that," he said, "the tempest has blowed something into my field. A kind of a ship I think it would be."

I was surprised at that until he explained that it was only a ghost ship and would do no hurt to the turnips. We argued that it had been blown up from the sea at Portsmouth, and then we talked of something else. There were two slates down at the parsonage and a big tree in Lumley's meadow. It was a rare storm.

I reckon the wind had blown our ghosts all over England. They were coming back for days afterwards with foundered horses and as footsore as possible, and they were so glad to get back to Fairfield that some of them walked up the street crying like little children. Squire said that his great-grandfather's great-grandfather hadn't looked so dead beat since the Battle of Naseby, and he's an educated man.

What with one thing and another, I should think it was a week before we got straight again, and then one afternoon I met the landlord on the green and he had a worried face. "I wish you'd come and have a look at that ship in my field," he said to me; "it seems to me it's leaning real hard on the turnips. I can't bear thinking what the missus will say when she sees it."

I walked down the lane with him, and sure enough there was a ship in the middle of his field, but such a ship as no man had seen on the water for three hundred years, let alone in the middle of a turnip field. It was all painted black and covered with carvings, and there was a great bay window in the stern for all the world like the squire's drawing room. There was a crowd of little black cannon on deck and looking out of her portholes, and she was anchored at each end to the hard ground. I have seen the wonders of the world on picture postcards, but I have never seen anything to equal that.

"She seems very solid for a ghost ship," I said, seeing the landlord was bothered.

"I should say it's a betwixt and between," he answered, puzzling it over, "but it's going to spoil a matter of fifty turnips, and missus she'll want it moved." We went up to her and touched the side, and it was as hard as a real ship. "Now there's folks in England would call that very curious," he said.

Now I don't know much about ships, but I should think that that ghost ship weighed a solid two hundred tons, and it seemed to me that she had come to stay, so that I felt sorry for the landlord, who was a married man. "All the horses in Fairfield won't move her out of my turnips," he said, frowning at her.

Just then we heard a noise on her deck, and we looked up and saw that a man had come out of her front cabin and was looking down at us very peaceably. He was dressed in a black uniform set out with rusty gold lace, and he had a great cutlass by his side in a brass sheath. "I'm Captain Bartholomew Roberts," he said, in a gentleman's voice, "put in for recruits. I seem to have brought her rather far up the harbor."

"Harbor!" cried landlord. "Why, you're fifty miles from the sea."

Captain Roberts didn't turn a hair. "So much as that, is it?" he said coolly. "Well, it's of no consequence."

Landlord was a bit upset at this. "I don't want to be unneighborly," he said, "but I wish you hadn't brought your ship into my field. You see, my wife sets great store on these turnips."

The captain took a pinch of snuff out of a fine gold box that he pulled out of his pocket, and dusted his fingers with a silk handkerchief in a very genteel fashion. "I'm only here for a few months," he said; "but if a testimony of my esteem would pacify your good lady I should be content," and with the words he loosed a great gold brooch from the neck of his coat and tossed it down to landlord.

Landlord blushed as red as a strawberry. "I'm not denying she's fond of jewelry," he said, "but it's too much for half a sackful of turnips." And indeed it was a handsome brooch.

The captain laughed. "Tut, man," he said, "it's a forced sale, and you deserve a good price. Say no more about it." And nodding good-day to us, he turned on his heel and went into the cabin. Landlord walked back up the lane like a man with a weight off his mind. "That tempest has blowed me a bit of luck," he said; "the missus will be main pleased with that brooch. It's better than blacksmith's guinea, any day."

Ninety-seven was Jubilee year, the year of the second Jubilee, you remember, and we had great doings at Fairfield, so that we hadn't much time to bother about the ghost ship, though anyhow it isn't our way to meddle in things that don't concern us. Landlord, he saw his tenant once or twice when he was hoeing his turnips and passed the time of day, and landlord's wife wore her new brooch to church every Sunday. But we didn't mix much with the ghosts at any time, all except an idiot lad there was in the village, and he didn't know the difference between a man and a ghost, poor innocent! On Jubilee Day, however, somebody told Captain Roberts why the church bells were ringing, and he hoisted a flag and fired off his guns like a loyal Englishman. 'Tis true the guns were shotted, and one of the round shot knocked a hole in farmer Johnstone's barn, but nobody thought much of that in such a season of rejoicing.

It wasn't till our celebrations were over that we noticed that anything was wrong in Fairfield. 'Twas shoemaker who told me first about it one morning at the "Fox and Grapes." "You know my great-great-uncle?" he said to me.

"You mean Joshua, the quiet lad," I answered, knowing him well.

"Quiet!" said shoemaker indignantly. "Quiet you call him, coming home at three o'clock every morning as drunk as a magistrate and waking up the whole house with his noise."

"Why, it can't be Joshua!" I said, for I knew him for one of the most respectable young ghosts in the village.

"Joshua it is," said shoemaker; "and one of these nights he'll find himself out in the street if he isn't careful."

This kind of talk shocked me, I can tell you, for I don't like to hear a man abusing his own family, and I could hardly believe that a steady youngster like Joshua had taken to drink. But just then in came butcher Aylwin in such a temper that he could hardly drink his beer. "The young puppy! The young puppy!" he kept on saying; and it was some time before shoemaker and I found out that he was talking about his ancestor that fell at Senlac.

"Drink?" said shoemaker hopefully, for we all like company in our misfortunes, and butcher nodded grimly.

"The young noodle," he said, emptying his tankard.

Well, after that I kept my ears open, and it was the same story all over the village. There was hardly a young man among all the ghosts of Fairfield who didn't roll home in the small hours of the morning the worse for liquor. I used to wake up in the night and hear them stumble past my house, singing outrageous songs. The worst of it was that we couldn't keep the scandal to ourselves, and the folk at Greenhill began to talk of "sodden Fairfield," and taught their children to sing a song about us:

> "Sodden Fairfield, sodden Fairfield, has no use
> for bread-and-butter;
> Rum for breakfast, rum for dinner, rum for tea,
> and rum for supper!"

We are easygoing in our village, but we didn't like that.

Of course we soon found out where the young fellows went to get the drink, and landlord was terribly cut up that his tenant should have turned out so badly, but his wife wouldn't hear of parting with the brooch, so that he couldn't give the captain notice to quit. But as time went on, things grew from bad to worse, and at all hours of the day you would see those young reprobates sleeping it off on the village green. Nearly every afternoon a ghost wagon used to jolt down to the ship with a lading of rum, and though the older ghosts seemed inclined to give the captain's hospitality the go-by, the youngsters were neither to hold nor to bind.

So one afternoon when I was taking my nap I heard a knock at the door, and there was parson looking very serious, like a man with a job before him that he didn't altogether relish. "I'm going down to talk to the captain about all this drunkenness in the village, and I want you to come with me," he said straight out.

I can't say that I fancied the visit much myself, and I tried to hint to parson that as, after all, they were only a lot of ghosts, it didn't very much matter.

"Dead or alive, I'm responsible for their good conduct," he said, "and I'm going to do my duty and put a stop to this continued disorder. And you are coming with me, John Simmons." So I went, parson being a persuasive kind of man.

We went down to the ship, and as we approached her I could see the captain tasting the air on deck. When he saw parson he took off his hat very politely, and I can tell you that I was relieved to find that he had a proper respect for the cloth. Parson acknowledged his salute and spoke out stoutly enough. "Sir, I should be glad to have a word with you."

"Come on board, sir; come on board," said the captain, and I could tell by his voice that he knew why we were there. Parson and I climbed up an uneasy kind of ladder, and the captain took us into the great cabin at the back of the ship, where the bay window was. It was the most wonderful place you ever saw in your life, all full of gold and silver plate, swords with jeweled scabbards, carved oak chairs, and great chests that looked as though they were bursting with guineas. Even parson was surprised, and he did not shake his head very hard when the captain took down some silver cups and poured us out a drink of rum. I tasted mine, and I don't mind saying that it changed my view of things entirely. There was nothing betwixt and between about that rum, and I felt that it was ridiculous to blame the lads for drinking too much of stuff like that. It seemed to fill my veins with honey and fire.

Parson put the case squarely to the captain, but I didn't listen much to what he said; I was busy sipping my drink and looking through the window at the fishes swimming to and fro over landlord's turnips. Just then it seemed the most natural thing in the world that they should be there, though afterwards, of course, I could see that that proved it was a ghost ship.

But even then I thought it was queer when I saw a drowned sailor float by in the thin air with his hair and beard all full of bubbles. It was the first time I had seen anything quite like that at Fairfield.

All the time I was regarding the wonders of the deep, parson was telling Captain Roberts how there was no peace or rest in the village owing to the curse of drunkenness, and what a bad example the youngsters were setting to the older ghosts. The captain listened very attentively, and only put in a word now and then about boys and young men sowing their wild oats. But when parson had finished his speech he filled up our silver cups and said to parson, with a flourish, "I should be sorry to cause trouble anywhere where I have been made welcome, and you will be glad to hear that I put to sea tomorrow night. And now you must drink me a prosperous voyage." So we all stood up and drank the toast with honor, and that noble rum was like hot oil in my veins.

After that captain showed us some of the curiosities he had brought back from foreign parts, and we were greatly amazed, though afterwards I couldn't clearly remember what they were. And then I found myself walking across the turnips with parson, and I was telling him of the glories of the deep that I had seen through the window of the ship. He turned on me severely. "If I were you, John Simmons," he said, "I should go straight home to bed." He has a way of putting things that wouldn't occur to an ordinary man, has parson, and I did as he told me.

Well, next day it came on to blow, and it blew harder and harder, till about eight o'clock at night I heard a noise and looked out into the garden. I daresay you won't believe me, it seems a bit tall even to me, but the wind had lifted the thatch of my pigsty into the widow's garden a second time. I thought I wouldn't wait to hear what widow had to say about it, so I went across the green to the "Fox and Grapes," and the wind was so strong that I danced along on tiptoe like a girl at the fair. When I got to the inn landlord had to help me shut the door; it seemed as though a dozen goats were pushing against it to come in out of the storm.

"It's a powerful tempest," he said, drawing the beer. "I hear there's a chimney down at Dickory End."

"It's a funny thing how these sailors know about the weather," I answered. "When captain said he was going tonight, I was thinking it would take a capful of wind to carry the ship back to sea, but now here's more than a capful."

"Ah, yes," said landlord, "it's tonight he goes true enough, and, mind you, though he treated me handsome over the rent, I'm not sure it's a loss to the village. I don't hold with gentrice who fetch their drink from London instead of helping local traders to get their living."

"But you haven't got any rum like his," I said, to draw him out.

His neck grew red above his collar, and I was afraid I'd gone too far; but after a while he got his breath with a grunt.

"John Simmons," he said, "if you've come down here

Sailing very comfortably through the windy stars

this windy night to talk a lot of fool's talk, you've wasted a journey."

Well, of course, then I had to smooth him down with praising his rum, and Heaven forgive me for swearing it was better than captain's. For the like of that rum no living lips have tasted save mine and parson's. But somehow or other I brought landlord round, and presently we must have a glass of his best to prove its quality.

"Beat that if you can!" he cried, and we both raised our glasses to our mouths, only to stop halfway and look at each other in amaze. For the wind that had been howling outside like an outrageous dog had all of a sudden turned as melodious as the carol boys of a Christmas Eve.

"Surely that's not my Martha," whispered landlord; Martha being his great-aunt that lived in the loft overhead.

We went to the door, and the wind burst it open so that the handle was driven clean into the plaster of the wall. But we didn't think about that at the time; for over our heads, sailing very comfortably through the windy stars, was the ship that had passed the summer in landlord's field. Her portholes and her bay window were blazing with lights, and there was a noise of singing and fiddling on her decks. "He's gone," shouted landlord above the storm, "and he's taken half the village with him!" I could only nod in answer, not having lungs like bellows of leather.

In the morning we were able to measure the strength of the storm, and over and above my pigsty there was damage enough wrought in the village to keep us busy. True it is that the children had to break down no branches for the firing that autumn, since the wind had strewn the woods with more than they could carry away. Many of our ghosts were scattered abroad, but this time very few came back, all the young men having sailed with captain; and not only ghosts, for a poor half-witted lad was missing, and we reckoned that he had stowed himself away or perhaps shipped as cabin boy, not knowing any better.

What with the lamentations of the ghost girls and the grumblings of families who had lost an ancestor, the village was upset for a while, and the funny thing was that it was the folk who had complained most of the carryings-on of the youngsters who made most noise now that they were gone. I hadn't any sympathy with shoemaker or butcher, who ran about saying how much they missed their lads, but it made me grieve to hear the poor bereaved girls calling their lovers by name on the village green at nightfall. It didn't seem fair to me that they should have lost their men a second time, after giving up life in order to join them, as like as not. Still, not even a spirit can be sorry forever, and after a few months we made up our mind that the folk who had sailed in the ship were never coming back, and we didn't talk about it any more.

And then one day, I daresay it would be a couple of years after, when the whole business was quite forgotten, who should come traipsing along the road from Portsmouth but the daft lad who had gone away with the ship without waiting till he was dead to become a ghost. You never saw such a boy as that in all your life. He had a great rusty cutlass hanging to a string at his waist, and he was tattooed all over in fine colors, so that even his face looked like a girl's sampler. He had a handkerchief in his hand full of foreign shells and old-fashioned pieces of small money, very curious, and he walked up to the well outside his mother's house and drew himself a drink as if he had been nowhere in particular.

The worst of it was that he had come back as softheaded as he went, and try as we might we couldn't get anything reasonable out of him. He talked a lot of gibberish about keelhauling and walking the plank and crimson murders—things which a decent sailor should know nothing about, so that it seemed to me that for all his manners captain had been more of a pirate than a gentleman mariner. But to draw sense out of that boy was as hard as picking cherries off a crab tree. One silly tale he had that he kept on drifting back to, and to hear him you would have thought that it was the only thing that happened to him in his life. "We was at anchor," he would say, "off an island called the Basket of Flowers, and the sailors had caught a lot of parrots and we were teaching them to swear. Up and down the decks, up and down the decks, and the language they used was dreadful. Then we looked up and saw the masts of the Spanish ship outside the harbor. Outside the harbor they were, so we threw the parrots into the sea and sailed out to fight. And all the parrots were drownded in the sea and the language they used was dreadful." That's the sort of boy he was, nothing but silly talk of parrots when we asked him about fighting. And we never had a chance of teaching him better, for two days after he ran away again, and hasn't been seen since.

That's my story, and I assure you that things like that are happening at Fairfield all the time. The ship has never come back, but somehow as people grow older they seem to think that one of these windy nights she'll come sailing in over the hedges with all the lost ghosts on board. Well, when she comes, she'll be welcome. There's one ghost lass that has never grown tired of waiting for her lad to return. Every night you'll see her out on the green, straining her poor eyes with looking for the mast lights among the stars. A faithful lass you'd call her, and I'm thinking you'd be right.

Landlord's field wasn't a penny the worse for the visit, but they do say that since then the turnips that have been grown in it have tasted of rum.

The Others

JOYCE CAROL OATES

EARLY ONE EVENING in a crowd of people, most of them commuters, he happened to see, quite by accident— he'd taken a slightly different route that day, having left the building in which he worked by an entrance he rarely used—and this, as he'd recall afterward, with the fussy precision which had characterized him since childhood, and helped to account for his success in his profession, because there was renovation being done in the main lobby—a man he had not seen in years, or was it decades: a face teasingly familiar, yet made strange by time, like an old photograph about to disintegrate into its elements.

Spence followed the man into the street, into a blowsy damp dusk, but did not catch up to him and introduce himself: that wasn't his way. He was certain he knew the man, and that the man knew him, but how, or why, or from what period in his life the man dated, he could not have said. Spence was forty-two years old and the other

seemed to be about that age, yet, oddly, older: his skin liv-
erish, his profile vague as if seen through an element
transparent yet dense, like water; his clothing—handsome
tweed overcoat, sharply creased gray trousers—hanging
slack on him, as if several sizes too large.

Outside, Spence soon lost sight of the man in a swarm
of pedestrians crossing the street; and made no effort to
locate him again. But for most of the ride home on the
train he thought of nothing else: who was that man, why
was he certain the man would have known him, what
were they to each other, resembling each other only very
slightly, yet close as twins? He felt stabs of excitement that
left him weak and breathless but it wasn't until that night,
when he and his wife were undressing for bed, that he said,
or heard himself say, in a voice of bemused wonder, and
dread: "I saw someone today who looked just like my
cousin Sandy—"

"Did I know Sandy?" his wife asked.

"—my cousin Sandy who died, who drowned, when we
were both in college."

"But did I know him?" his wife asked. She cast him an
impatient sidelong glance and smiled her sweet-derisive
smile. "It's difficult to envision him if I've never seen him,
and if he's been dead for so long, why should it matter so
much to you?"

Spence had begun to perspire. His heart beat hard and
steady as if in the presence of danger. "I don't understand
what you're saying," he said.

Miss Reuter

"The actual words, or their meaning?"

"The words."

She laughed as if he had said something witty, and did not answer him. As he fell asleep he tried not to think of his cousin Sandy whom he had not seen in twenty years and whom he'd last seen in an open casket in a funeral home in Damascus, Minnesota.

The second episode occurred a few weeks later when Spence was in line at a post office, not the post office he usually frequented but another, larger, busier, in a suburban township adjacent to his own, and the elderly woman in front of him drew his attention: wasn't she, too, someone he knew? Or had known, many years ago? He stared, fascinated, at her stitched-looking skin, soft and puckered as a glove of some exquisite material, and unnaturally white; her eyes that were small, sunken, yet shining; her astonishing hands—delicate, even skeletal, discolored by liver spots like coins, yet with rings on several fingers, and in a way rather beautiful. The woman appeared to be in her midnineties, if not older: fussy, anxious, very possibly addled: complaining ceaselessly to herself, or to others by way of herself. Yet her manner was mirthful; nervous bustling energy crackled about her like invisible bees.

He believed he knew who she was: Miss Reuter, a teacher of his in elementary school. Whom he had not seen in more years than he wanted to calculate.

Miss Reuter, though enormously aged, was able, it

seemed, to get around by herself. She carried a large rather glitzy shopping bag made of a silvery material, and in this bag, and in another at her feet, she was rummaging for her change purse, as she called it, which she could not seem to find. The post office clerk waited with a show of strained patience; the line now consisted of a half-dozen people.

Spence asked Miss Reuter—for surely it was she: while virtually unrecognizable she was at the same time unmistakable—if she needed some assistance. He did not call her by name and as she turned to him, in exasperation, and gratitude—as if she knew that he, or someone, would come shortly to her aid—she did not seem to recognize him. Spence paid for her postage and a roll of stamps and Miss Reuter, still rummaging in her bag, vexed, cheerful, befuddled, thanked him without looking up at him. She insisted it must be a loan, and not a gift, for she was, she said, "not yet an object of public charity."

Afterward Spence put the incident out of his mind, knowing the woman was dead. It was purposeless to think of it, and would only upset him.

After that he began to see them more frequently. The Others—as he thought of them. On the street, in restaurants, at church; in the building in which he worked; on the very floor, in the very department, in which his office was located. (He was a tax lawyer for one of the largest of American "conglomerates"—yes and very well paid.) One morning his wife saw him standing at a bedroom window looking out toward the street. She poked him playfully in the ribs. "What's wrong?" she said. "None of this behavior suits you."

"There's someone out there, at the curb."

"No one's there."

"I have the idea he's waiting for me."

"Oh yes, I do see someone," his wife said carelessly. "He's often there. But I doubt that he's waiting for you."

She laughed, as at a private joke. She was a pretty freckled snub-nosed woman given to moments of mysterious amusement. Spence had married her long ago in a trance of love from which he had yet to awaken.

Spence said, his voice shaking, "I think—I'm afraid I think I might be having a nervous breakdown. I'm so very, very afraid."

"No," said his wife, "—you're the sanest person I know. All surface and no cracks, fissures, potholes."

Spence turned to her. His eyes were filling with tears.

"Don't joke. Have pity."

She made no reply; seemed about to drift away; then slipped an arm around his waist and nudged her head against his shoulder in a gesture of camaraderie. Whether mocking, or altogether genuine, Spence could not have said.

"It's just that I'm so afraid."

"Yes, you've said."

"—of losing my mind. Going mad."

She stood for a moment, peering out toward the street. The elderly gentleman standing at the curb glanced back but could not have seen them, or anyone, behind the lacy bedroom curtains. He was well dressed, and carried an umbrella. An umbrella? Perhaps it was a cane.

Spence said, "I seem to be seeing, more and more, these people—people I don't think are truly there."

"*He's* there."

"I think they're dead. Dead people."

His wife drew back and cast him a sidelong glance, smiling mysteriously. "It does seem to have upset you," she said.

"Since I know they're not there—"

"*He's* there."

"—so I must be losing my mind. A kind of schizophrenia, waking dreams, hallucinations—"

Spence was speaking excitedly, and did not know exactly what he was saying. His wife drew away from him in alarm, or distaste.

"You take everything so personally," she said.

One morning shortly after the New Year, when the air was sharp as a knife and the sky so blue it brought tears of pain to one's eyes, Spence set off on the underground route from his train station to his building. Beneath the city's paved surface was a honeycomb of tunnels, some of them damp and befouled but most of them in good condition, with, occasionally, a corridor of gleaming white tiles that looked as if it had been lovingly polished by hand. Spence preferred aboveground, or believed he should prefer aboveground, for reasons vague and puritanical, but in fierce weather he made his way underground, and worried only that he might get lost, as he sometimes did. (Yet, even lost, he had only to find an escalator or steps leading to the street—and he was no longer lost.)

This morning, however, the tunnels were far more crowded than usual. Spence saw a preponderance of elderly men and women, with here and there a young face, startling, and seemingly unnatural. Here and there, yet more startling, a child's face. Very few of the faces had that air, so disconcerting to him in the past, of the eerily familiar laid upon the utterly unfamiliar; and these he resolutely ignored.

He soon fell into step with the crowd, keeping to their pace—which was erratic, surging, faster along straight stretches of tunnel and slower at curves; he found it agreeable to be borne along by the flow, as of a tide. A tunnel of familiar tearstained mosaics yielded to one of the smart gleaming tunnels and that in turn to a tunnel badly in need of repair—and, indeed, being noisily repaired, by one of those crews of workmen that labor at all hours of the day and night beneath the surface of the city—and as Spence hurried past the deafening vibrations of the air hammer he found himself descending stairs into a tunnel unknown to him: a place of warm, humming, droning sound, like conversation, though none of his fellow pedestrians seemed to be talking. Where were they going, so many people? And in the same direction?—with only, here and there, a lone, clearly lost individual bucking the tide, white-faced, eyes snatching at his as if in desperate recognition.

Might as well accompany them, Spence thought, and see.

AFTERWORD

Few tales capture the imagination as thoroughly as great ghost stories. Whether told around a roaring campfire or by the light of a single flickering candle, tales of visitors from the beyond are guaranteed to send shivers down the back of even the most fearless readers and listeners.

In this collection of—appropriately enough—thirteen ghostly tales, master illustrator Barry Moser has assembled an assortment of ghoulish and chilling tales by some of the greatest storytellers of the past century and a half. From Bram Stoker's "The Judge's House," Arthur Conan Doyle's "How It Happened," and the traditional British ballad "Polly Vaughn" (retold by Moser himself) through H. G. Wells's "The Red Room," E. Nesbit's "Man-Size in Marble," and H. P. Lovecraft's "The Music of Erich Zann" and right up to such modern stories as Joyce Carol Oates's "The Others," Madeleine L'Engle's "Poor Little Saturday," and Philippa Pearce's "Samantha and the Ghost," this collection demonstrates the breadth and depth of the art of the ghost story.

There are few people as ideally suited to selecting and illustrating such a collection as Barry Moser. His haunting paintings and wood engravings for *Frankenstein* and *Tales of Edgar Allan Poe* are among the most brilliant and memorable illustrations ever created for these masterworks of the macabre. In each of his fifteen watercolor paintings for this collection, Moser's affinity for the supernatural—from the eerily lit flying galleon to the ominous gnarled monkey's paw to the vision of fear in the old violinist's eyes—can clearly be seen.

Combining spine-tingling tales of terror with his own compelling visions of the supernatural, Moser has created a book that is sure to invite readers of all ages back time and again to explore the chilling delights of these great ghost stories.

—Peter Glassman

ABOUT THE AUTHORS

ARTHUR CONAN DOYLE (1859–1930) elevated the detective story to a genre of its own with the creation of Sherlock Holmes. A former physician, Conan Doyle wrote everything from plays to poetry, historical novels to scholarly works. To his great regret, it was the confident, hyperlogical Holmes for whom the public clamored. Conan Doyle devoted the final fifteen years of his life to advancing the cause of spiritualism—the belief that spirits of the dead communicate with the living.

JAMES HASKINS grew up within a family of storytellers. He is a professor and the award-winning author of more than one hundred books for children and adults, many of which focus on African Americans and their heritage. Haskins most recently compiled *Moaning Bones: African-American Ghost Stories,* retellings of oral tales originally collected by folklorists in the 1920s and 1930s.

W[ILLIAM] W[YMARK] JACOBS (1863–1943) was in his lifetime chiefly recognized for his humorous short stories, many of which feature surprise endings. Today he is best known for "The Monkey's Paw," which has been adapted for stage and screen.

MADELEINE L'ENGLE has written in many genres, for both children and adults. She is best known for her Newbery Award–winning *A Wrinkle in Time,* a story that combines science fiction, fantasy, and philosophy. The rich fantasy worlds L'Engle began creating as a child have led her to become one of the most popular children's authors in the world.

H[OWARD] P[HILLIPS] LOVECRAFT (1890–1937) is widely acknowledged to be the twentieth century's most important writer of supernatural fiction. His own first efforts at horror writing followed his reading, at age eight, of the tales of Edgar Allan Poe. Lovecraft's "weird tales" are renowned for their ability to conjure bizarre dimensions and instill a sense of imminent dread.

RICHARD MIDDLETON (1882–1911) was a magazine contributor, poet, and essayist whose work was not published in book form until after his death. Middleton's stories are praised for their unique blend of humor and the uncanny, a combination epitomized in "The Ghost Ship," his most famous story.

E[DITH] NESBIT (1858–1924) wrote in many genres, but she is best known for her children's literature. Her stories—both realistic and fantasy—are acclaimed for their imagination, detail, and humor. Nesbit's magical adventure stories were among the first that sought simply to entertain young readers, rather than teach them lessons.

JOYCE CAROL OATES has been described as "a master storyteller of the dark side." A professor at Princeton University and the author of numerous novels, short stories, plays, poems, and essays, Oates won the National Book Award for her novel *them* and has won several O. Henry awards for her short fiction. Her recent works include *Haunted: Tales of the Grotesque* and the compilation *H. P. Lovecraft: Major Works*.

PHILIPPA PEARCE, winner of the Carnegie Medal for her novel *Tom's Midnight Children,* has written a number of ghost stories for children. Collections of her stories include *The Shadow Cage: And Other Tales of the Supernatural* and *Who's Afraid? And Other Strange Stories.*

BRAM STOKER (1847–1912) began writing ghost stories as a child, inspired by the grisly tales his mother told to entertain him. As an adult, Stoker also wrote novels of adventure and romance, but he is most famous for his vampire tale, *Dracula,* which has not gone out of print since its first publication, in 1897.

CATHERINE WELLS (1872–1927) published only a few short stories in her lifetime. In an effort to achieve literary success apart from her husband, H. G. Wells, she submitted her work to periodicals through agents and from various addresses. After her death, Mr. Wells published a collection of her stories as a tribute.

H[ERBERT] G[EORGE] WELLS (1866–1946) was one of the most prolific and versatile writers of his time. He is best known for the science fiction classics *The War of the Worlds, The Time Machine, The Invisible Man,* and *The Island of Doctor Moreau,* but he also composed college textbooks, political treatises, and children's books. Many of his works of fiction concern the macabre and supernatural.

OZ TITLES IN THE
Books of Wonder Series

THE WONDERFUL WIZARD OF OZ
by L. Frank Baum
with 24 full-color plates and over 130 two-color illustrations
by W. W. Denslow

THE MARVELOUS LAND OF OZ
by L. Frank Baum
with 16 full-color plates and over 125 black-and-white illustrations
by John R. Neill

OZMA OF OZ
by L. Frank Baum
with 42 full-color plates and 21 two-color illustrations
by John R. Neill

DOROTHY AND THE WIZARD IN OZ
by L. Frank Baum
with 16 full-color plates and 50 black-and-white illustrations
by John R. Neill

THE ROAD TO OZ
by L. Frank Baum
with 126 black-and-white illustrations on multicolored paper
by John R. Neill

THE EMERALD CITY OF OZ
by L. Frank Baum
with 16 full-color plates and 90 black-and-white illustrations
by John R. Neill

THE PATCHWORK GIRL OF OZ
by L. Frank Baum
with 51 full-color and 80 black-and-white illustrations
by John R. Neill

TIK-TOK OF OZ
by L. Frank Baum
with 12 full-color plates and 78 black-and-white illustrations
by John R. Neill

THE SCARECROW OF OZ
by L. Frank Baum
with 12 full-color plates and 104 black-and-white illustrations
by John R. Neill

RINKITINK IN OZ
by L. Frank Baum
with 12 full-color plates and 97 black-and-white illustrations
by John R. Neill

THE LOST PRINCESS OF OZ
by L. Frank Baum
with 12 full-color plates and 98 black-and-white illustrations
by John R. Neill

LITTLE WIZARD STORIES OF OZ
by L. Frank Baum
with 45 full-color illustrations
by John R. Neill

DOROTHY OF OZ
by Roger S. Baum
with full-color frontispiece and 50 black-and-white illustrations
by Elizabeth Miles

If you enjoy the Oz books and want to know more about Oz, you may be interested in The Royal Club of Oz. Devoted to America's favorite fairyland, it is a club for everyone who loves the Oz books. For free information, please send a first-class stamp to:

The Royal Club of Oz
P.O. Box 714
New York, New York 10011
or call toll free: (800) 207-6968

BOOKS OF WONDER CLASSICS

DELUXE GIFT EDITIONS OF TIMELESS STORIES, LAVISHLY ILLUSTRATED
WITH FULL-COLOR PLATES AND BLACK-AND-WHITE DRAWINGS

THE ARABIAN NIGHTS
retold by Brian Alderson
illustrated by Michael Foreman

ALICE'S ADVENTURES IN WONDERLAND
by Lewis Carroll
illustrated by John Tenniel

THROUGH THE LOOKING-GLASS
by Lewis Carroll
illustrated by John Tenniel

THE TROJAN WAR AND THE ADVENTURES OF ODYSSEUS
by Padraic Colum
illustrated by Barry Moser

A CHRISTMAS CAROL
by Charles Dickens
illustrated by Carter Goodrich

OLIVER TWIST
by Charles Dickens
illustrated by Don Freeman

THE ADVENTURES OF SHERLOCK HOLMES
by Sir Arthur Conan Doyle
illustrated by Barry Moser

THE WHITE COMPANY
by Sir Arthur Conan Doyle
illustrated by N. C. Wyeth

THE THREE MUSKETEERS
by Alexandre Dumas
illustrated by Tom Kidd

THE MAGICAL LAND OF NOOM
written and illustrated by Johnny Gruelle

THE GIFT OF THE MAGI
by O. Henry
illustrated by Michael Dooling

THE LEGEND OF SLEEPY HOLLOW
by Washington Irving
illustrated by Arthur Rackham

RIP VAN WINKLE
by Washington Irving
illustrated by N. C. Wyeth

THE WATER-BABIES
by Charles Kingsley
illustrated by Jessie Willcox Smith

THE JUNGLE BOOK
by Rudyard Kipling
illustrated by Jerry Pinkney

JUST SO STORIES
by Rudyard Kipling
illustrated by Barry Moser

THE RAINBOW FAIRY BOOK
by Andrew Lang
illustrated by Michael Hague

THE STORY OF DOCTOR DOLITTLE
by Hugh Lofting
illustrated by Michael Hague

AT THE BACK OF THE NORTH WIND
by George MacDonald
illustrated by Jessie Willcox Smith

THE PRINCESS AND THE GOBLIN
by George MacDonald
illustrated by Jessie Willcox Smith

GREAT GHOST STORIES
selected and illustrated by Barry Moser

THE ENCHANTED CASTLE
by E. Nesbit
illustrated by Paul O. Zelinsky

TALES OF EDGAR ALLAN POE
by Edgar Allan Poe
illustrated by Barry Moser

BLACK BEAUTY
by Anna Sewell
illustrated by Lucy Kemp-Welch

HEIDI
by Johanna Spyri
illustrated by Jessie Willcox Smith

A CHILD'S GARDEN OF VERSES
by Robert Louis Stevenson
illustrated by Diane Goode

THE ADVENTURES OF HUCKLEBERRY FINN
by Mark Twain
illustrated by Steven Kellogg

THE ADVENTURES OF TOM SAWYER
by Mark Twain
illustrated by Barry Moser

A CONNECTICUT YANKEE IN KING ARTHUR'S COURT
by Mark Twain
illustrated by Trina Schart Hyman

AROUND THE WORLD IN EIGHTY DAYS
by Jules Verne
illustrated by Barry Moser

REBECCA OF SUNNYBROOK FARM
by Kate Douglas Wiggin
illustrated by Helen Mason Grose

THE HAPPY PRINCE AND OTHER STORIES
by Oscar Wilde
illustrated by Charles Robinson